Stairstep Farm
Anna Rose's Story

Titles in the Polish American Girls Series:

Stairstep Farm:
Anna Rose's Story

by Anne Pellowski

Pictures by Wendy Watson

Saint Mary's Press
Christian Brothers Publications
Winona, Minnesota

Genuine recycled paper with 10% post-consumer waste.
Printed with soy-based ink.

The publishing team included Stephan Nagel, development editor and cover
designer; Jacqueline M. Captain, copy editor; Alan S. Hanson, production editor; Maurine R. Twait, art director; Kent Linder, graphic designer; pre-press,
printing, and binding by the graphics division of Saint Mary's Press.

Republished by Saint Mary's Press, 1998. Originally published by the Putnam
Publishing Group. Used with permission.

Printed in the United States of America

Printing: 9 8 7 6 5 4 3 2 1

Year: 2006 05 04 03 02 01 00 99 98

ISBN 0-88489-536-X

Cataloging information
Pellowski, Anne, author. Watson, Wendy, illustrator.
Title: Stairstep Farm: Anna Rose's Story
Summary: Anna Rose is not sure how she feels about all the attention the new
baby is getting. But her life as a Polish Catholic in rural Wisconsin is filled with
family and busy with farmwork. Anna Rose and the other children can make
almost any chore an occasion for fun. Intended for grades 3–5.

1. Polish Americans—Juvenile fiction. 2. Farm life—Juvenile fiction. 3. Wisconsin—Trempealeau County—History—Juvenile fiction. 4. Minnesota—Winona
County—History—Juvenile fiction.

Contents

To my brother and sisters

Brown Betty

"Meow, meow, meow!" Anna Rose woke up to the faint sound of a hungry kitten, crying for its milk. She poked her head out from beneath the feather quilt, and saw her oldest sister, Angie, standing over the heat register in the floor, getting dressed as fast as she could. It was a cold January morning. There was no furnace in their house, only a big, round stove in the front room and the black and white range in the kitchen. In the ceiling right above the front room stove was a square hole, covered with metal grating. Quite a bit of heat went up through this hole into the bedroom above, where Anna Rose slept with her two younger sisters, Janie and Mary Elizabeth. Angie and Millie, her two older sisters, slept in the room next to it. In winter, they always came and stood on the register to get dressed.

"Maaah, maaah, maaah!" This time the crying sounded more like a little calf.

"Is that a kitten or a calf crying like that?" Anna Rose asked Angie.

"Why don't you get dressed and come down and see," laughed Angie as she went to give Millie a shake to wake her up.

"Time to get up for chores!"

While Millie struggled out of bed and into her clothes, Anna Rose snuggled back under the fat, puffy quilt that was filled with goose feathers. Mary Elizabeth was sleeping in the middle of the bed, curled up in a ball. She had only started to sleep upstairs since Christmas. Sometimes she crawled in between Angie and Millie, and slept with them, but most nights she slept between Anna Rose and Janie.

"Myah, myah, myah!" Again the crying sound came up through the register.

"I've got to find out what that is," Anna Rose said as she took the leap out of bed, raced for the register, grabbed her clothes from a chair nearby, and dressed as fast as she could. Over her thick, long underwear she pulled on her long stockings and then her shoes. Down the steps she clattered, opening the door to the kitchen.

She stopped in surprise. She had expected to see her mother standing at the stove, getting breakfast ready. But instead, there was her cousin, Dorothy, smiling at her as though she had a secret.

"What are *you* doing here?" Anna Rose asked. Dorothy hadn't been there when she went to bed the evening before.

"Don't you know why? Haven't you been hearing some strange noises?" Dorothy seemed to be teasing her.

"Yes, I heard something crying like a kitten or a calf. Where is it?" Anna Rose looked all around the kitchen, but could see no animal.

"You knew your mother was expecting a baby, didn't you?" Dorothy spoke in a voice that seemed to indicate she meant just the opposite. Anna Rose was not going to admit that she hadn't known any such thing. She had suspected something like that might happen, but no one had told her definitely that there would be a new baby around their house.

"Myeh, myeh, myeh!" The crying started up again. Anna Rose could hear that it came from the big downstairs bedroom where Mama and Daddy slept. But it didn't sound like a baby crying—it sounded like a kitten or a newborn calf.

Suddenly, Anna Rose imagined her mother lying in bed, with a row of kittens lined up beside her. What if, instead of having a baby, she had had a kitten, or even worse, a whole litter of kittens! Could such a terrible thing happen?

"There are no kittens in the house, are there?" Anna Rose asked anxiously.

Dorothy glanced up from her cooking with a questioning look. She saw the worried frown on Anna Rose's face.

"No," she said with a reassuring laugh. "There is only a new baby, a girl—your new sister. Sometimes when she cries she might sound like a kitten, but she's not. She's a tiny little girl, just like you were once. I'll take you in to see her after breakfast."

Anna Rose sighed with relief. Kittens and calves were

all right in the barn, but she didn't want to see her mother cuddling and nursing them, like she used to do with Mary Elizabeth.

Dorothy put the oatmeal on the back of the stove.

"If that starts to bubble over, call me. I'm going upstairs to get the little ones up and dressed."

Anna Rose watched the pot of oatmeal, but nothing happened. The heat from the back of the kitchen stove was too weak to make it boil over. Soon Dorothy came down, carrying Mary Elizabeth and holding Janie by the hand. She set Mary Elizabeth in the high chair and put Janie down on a regular chair with a pillow on it. Just as she was dishing out the oatmeal, Angie and Millie came in with big armloads of wood and dropped them into the bin on the side wall. That was one of their jobs every morning. In the late afternoon, they had to bring in more wood for both stoves.

"Can we go in and see her now?" asked Angie excitedly.

"No, wait till you've all had breakfast," Dorothy replied, dishing out more bowls of oatmeal. No sooner had she done that, when Daddy and Lawrence and Francis walked in the kitchen door. They had just finished the milking.

Francis took off his thick woolen cap and his red curls tumbled out, sticking up every which way. His hair was the same color as Janie's, and just as curly. Grown-ups always admired Janie's curls and stroked her head, saying: "My, doesn't she have lovely hair!" But for some reason, they didn't say that about Francis's hair. They would tease him instead, and call him "Carrot-Top" or "Curly-Head." Anna Rose always wondered why they didn't say the same things about *his* hair as they said about Janie's.

Lawrence was almost four years older than Francis. On his next birthday, he would be sixteen, but already he was taller than Daddy. When the other farmers living near them saw Lawrence standing next to Daddy they always said: "So, Alex, you're raising another one of those giants." That was because Grandpa and Daddy's uncles were all so tall and big.

Lawrence had smooth, dark-red hair and as he took off his cap with the earflaps, he ran his fingers through it to push it back, away from his eyes.

"Well, Anna Rose, what do you think of our new sister?" asked Lawrence.

"She thought it was a kitten," interrupted Dorothy with a chuckle.

"I did not!" protested Anna Rose. "I just thought I *heard* a kitten." She hated it when they made fun of her about something she was supposed to know.

After breakfast, they went in, one by one, to see their new sister. She was almost as tiny as a kitten, but she was definitely a baby, with head, eyes, nose, and mouth and hands. She wasn't crying any more because she was sound asleep. Mama was dozing, too.

Later that morning, everyone went to church except Mama and the new baby and Dorothy.

"Are we going in the sleigh?" asked Anna Rose. When there was a lot of fresh snow their car couldn't make it up the hill, not even with chains on the tires. Then Daddy and Lawrence would hitch up King and Dollie, two of the horses, to the long wagon box placed on top of runners. They called it their sleigh. On the floor of the wagon box was a thick layer of hay, to make it warm and comfortable to sit. They also took along plenty of blankets to cover their legs and feet. Even though the wagon box was open, and not warmed by a heater like their car, they all loved to go to church in it, sliding smoothly along behind the team.

"No, I think we'll make out all right with the car," said Daddy. "We have to get back as soon as we can, to give Dorothy a hand. A new baby is a lot of work."

"I'll try to have dinner ready by the time you get back," said Dorothy. "I'm planning a special treat of Brown Betty. You all like that, don't you?" Dorothy turned to the younger children with a questioning smile.

Anna Rose did not know what Brown Betty was. She had never heard her mother mention it. It sounded interesting, but she was not so sure she would like it. Anyway, she was disappointed that they were not going in the sleigh. She was also jealous of all the attention being given her new sister.

"I don't like Brown Betty," announced Anna Rose.

"Don't like Betty," said Mary Elizabeth. She had learned to talk in sentences a few weeks ago and now she repeated part of everything that Anna Rose or Janie said.

Janie looked as though she might say she didn't like Brown Betty either, but Lawrence interrupted before she could speak.

"That's good you two don't like Brown Betty pudding, because that leaves more for me. I *love* it!" Lawrence smacked his lips as he went out the door.

"Yum, yum, I do, too!" Angie rubbed her stomach. Millie did the same. Soon they were all talking about how good Brown Betty pudding was.

"I didn't know it was a pudding," Anna Rose said to herself. She liked most puddings, but especially chocolate. "Goodness," she thought, "chocolate is brown. What if Brown Betty is a kind of chocolate pudding? And I won't get to eat any because I said I didn't like it." She almost changed her mind and said she really did like Brown Betty a little, but she was too stubborn and cross to admit it.

"I don't like Brown Betty," she insisted.

All during Mass, Anna Rose thought about Brown Betty pudding. She thought about it on the way home in the car. The chains on the back tires thonked softly at each turn of the wheels. "Brown Betty," "Brown Betty," "Brown Betty," they seemed to be saying.

When they got back to the house, there was a delicious smell of roast chicken and apples spreading throughout the kitchen. Wisps of steam curled up from the crusty brown chunks covering a big, flat pan set in the middle of the kitchen table. Dorothy must have taken the pan out of the oven a few minutes before.

"Um-mm!" Lawrence leaned over the pan and took a deep sniff. "I *love* that Brown Betty!"

"Set the table, Millie. Angie, you can help me by stirring this gravy until it gets thick. Lawrence, why don't you mash the potatoes for me, over there by the sink. Francis, run down and get some more milk from the cellar." Dorothy gave orders left and right while she brought out the bread board and began to slice a fat, rounded loaf of the bread Mama had baked yesterday. Then she fixed up a plate of food and took it into the bedroom where Mama still lay in bed, with the new baby beside her. Anna Rose peeked in to see if Mama was sick. Mama was sitting up, with the pillows behind her. She looked tired, but not sick and feverish, the way she had looked once when she had stayed in bed with the flu.

The rest of the family sat around the table in the kitchen and ate dinner. They were too hungry to say much. After they had finished the chicken and mashed potatoes and gravy and yellow beans, Dorothy cleared the plates away and brought out a stack of small bowls. With a serving spoon, she dished out the Brown Betty from the pan. From another bowl she plopped a big spoonful of whipped cream onto each portion, and then passed the bowls around.

At the bottom and top of the Brown Betty was a crispy, crumbly crust and in the middle were sliced apples and applesauce, with cinnamon and raisins. It didn't look like a pudding, but it did smell delicious.

Mary Elizabeth and Janie each wanted a bowl. They started to eat their portions, smacking their lips as Lawrence had done. Dorothy held out a bowl in front of Anna Rose and gave her a questioning look. Anna Rose shook her head.

"I don't like Brown Betty."

"All right. That was your last chance." Dorothy scooped up the remaining portions of the Brown Betty and spooned them into Lawrence's and Francis's bowls. They had already finished their first helpings and wanted seconds. Anna Rose watched as they gobbled up the Brown Betty. Now she would never know how it tasted. She felt the tears coming and blinked hard so she wouldn't cry. Angie jumped up at that moment.

"Come on, Millie, let's get these dishes done so we can go hold the baby for a while."

"I'll dry the knives and forks and spoons," offered Anna Rose. She thought that might help her forget about the Brown Betty.

Angie and Millie finished their washing and drying, but Anna Rose still had a pile of knives and forks to dry. She liked to do all the spoons first, then the knives, and last of all the forks, because they were hardest to get dry between all the tines. Millie started to help her but Anna Rose said: "Don't! I want to do them by myself."

14

On the other side of the kitchen, Daddy was sitting in the rocking chair, with Mary Elizabeth on one knee. He was bouncing her and singing a tune. Janie was about to get up on the other knee when she ran to the front room, and came back with a harmonica. She handed it to Daddy. He put it to his mouth and began to play. It was a Polish song they all knew, about a gray horse and sleigh:

> *Śiwy koń, śiwy koń,*
> *Malowany sankie,*
> *Poja dem, poja dem,*
> *Do twója kochankie.*

> Little gray horse, little
>   gray horse,
> Brightly painted sleigh,
> Move along, move along,
> To your little darling.

In the front room, Lawrence, Francis, Angie, and Millie began to sing along. Softly, Anna Rose joined them as she continued wiping the knives. It was such a jolly song that she began to forget all about the Brown Betty. Then Daddy played another lively song, about a rabbit. When that was finished, he started another, also about a rabbit, but slower and not as bouncy. At the part where the rabbit disappeared, Daddy made the harmonica sound full of sorrow:

> *Byl to kot?*
> *Byl to kot?*

> Was it the cat?
> Was it the cat?

The harmonica wailed mournfully, sounding so much like a person crying that Anna Rose couldn't stop herself from bursting into tears. Daddy looked over at her in surprise, and then at Mary Elizabeth and Janie. They looked like they might start crying any minute.

"Did I make you so sad?" Daddy wondered. "We'll see about that!" He got up from the rocker, and holding the harmonica in one hand and Mary Elizabeth in the other, he started to play a lively polka. Round and round he twirled her, from the kitchen into the front room and back again. His feet made skipping hops as he turned. Mary Elizabeth crowed and chuckled and gasped with laughter.

"Now me," pleaded Janie when Daddy stopped to get his breath. She held up her arms to show that she wanted a dance. He put Mary Elizabeth down in the rocker, picked up Janie, and then started playing another polka. Hop, skip, turn! Hop, skip, turn! Round and round he went with Janie.

Anna Rose finished her wiping to the beat of the music. Wipe, wipe, wipe! Wipe, wipe, wipe! She moved the dishcloth back and forth over the tines. When her father came to a stop in the kitchen he was panting. Anna Rose wanted a dance with him, too, but she was afraid he would think she was a baby if she asked to be held in his arms.

"Do you want to dance, too?" asked Daddy, and without waiting for her answer, he leaned down and put his arm around Anna Rose's waist. He was dancing with her just the way he did with Mama! Whirling and twirling they went from the kitchen to the front room and back again. Sometimes Daddy lifted Anna Rose right off the floor as he swung her around. When the tune came to an end, he set her down by the kitchen table.

Anna Rose had to lean against the table for a while, she was so dizzy. Then she saw that she had forgotten to put away the knives and forks and spoons. She took a bunch of knives in one hand and the forks in the other, and went straight to the drawer in the pantry where they were supposed to go. As she placed them in the right spaces, Anna Rose noticed a small round pan on top of the counter. It smelled of Brown Betty. She was not quite tall enough to see over the rim, so she gently poked a finger into the pan. It touched a crumbly crust.

Quickly, Anna Rose went back to the kitchen to look around. No one was paying attention to her. She took the bunch of spoons and a small stool that was kept under the sink for her and Janie to stand on when they wanted a drink of water.

Anna Rose put the stool next to the cupboards, dropped all but one spoon in the drawer, and then pulled the pan close to the counter edge, right in front of her nose. The Brown Betty looked crusty and brown. It was still warm.

"If I take a bite and then smooth it over, no one will notice," thought Anna Rose. She dipped the spoon into the Brown Betty, and brought it up, full and dripping, into her mouth. How good it tasted! Crunchy and chewy on the outside and soft and sweet on the inside. She took another bite, then another. She saw the bottom of the pan showing through! She wanted to take another bite but she didn't dare. Dorothy must be saving this pan for something special. Carefully, she scooped out some of the inside filling from around the hole she had made and smoothed it over the hole. She spread the crumbly topping as best she could.

"It looks just the same as before," Anna Rose whispered, trying to convince herself that it was true. She got down off the stool and went back into the kitchen. Daddy was still in the rocking chair, resting after his wild dancing, and playing softly on the harmonica. Mary Elizabeth sat on one knee and Janie on the other.

In the front room, Angie and Millie were taking turns holding the new baby, while Dorothy watched them. Lawrence and Francis had started a game of checkers. From the back bedroom, Mama called out something, but so faintly Anna Rose could not hear.

"All right, I'll bring it," Dorothy answered.

Dorothy came into the kitchen and got out a cup and saucer and one of the small glass bowls. She poured coffee into the cup.

"Time for your Mama to have the Brown Betty I saved for her," said Dorothy. "You can help me carry it in. Save that spoon you're wiping, and take it along."

Anna Rose held her breath as Dorothy went into the pantry. She heard the scraping sound of the spoon, scooping the Brown Betty from the pan into the bowl. When Dorothy came out she handed the bowl to Anna Rose.

"Here, you carry this and I'll carry the coffee," directed Dorothy.

Anna Rose could hardly hold the glass dish, she felt so weak with relief that Dorothy hadn't noticed anything.

"This looks good," said Mama when they got to the bedroom. "You'll have to give me the recipe. I've never made Brown Betty."

Dorothy glanced at Anna Rose, gave a big smile, and left the room. Mama began to take small bites of Brown Betty and then sips of coffee. She had almost emptied the dish when she put it down.

"I'm too full. You eat the rest," Mama said.

Anna Rose gobbled up the last spoonfuls. It was so good! When she took the dish to the kitchen sink, she said not a word to Dorothy.

For a few more weeks, Dorothy stayed with them, helping Mama with the housework. Their new sister was baptized one Sunday, and named Virginia, but everyone except Mama called her Virgie.

The day before she left, Dorothy made Brown Betty again. She put a dish in front of Anna Rose.

"Now you like it, don't you?" Dorothy prodded her.

Anna Rose was still too stubborn to admit she was wrong. She *didn't* want to say she liked it, yet, she *did* want some Brown Betty to eat.

"Mama says we have to eat whatever is put on the table," said Anna Rose as she picked up the dish of Brown Betty and began to eat it, pretending that she didn't like it. Dorothy laughed, but she didn't say anything.

"Next time," thought Anna Rose, "I'd better look to see what it is before I say I don't like it."

19

Anniversary Party

On the first Sunday in February the whole family went to church. Dorothy was no longer with them, but it was still a tight squeeze getting everyone into the car. Grandma and Grandpa had had their fifty-fourth wedding anniversary a few days ago, but it was being celebrated today.

In church, they sat behind Grandpa, Aunt Sophie, Uncle Roman, and their children: Imelda, Sally Ann, Anthony, and Mabel. Grandma was not there because she could not walk around any more. For a few months she had been sick in bed and never got up.

On the back of the pew in front of him, Grandpa had hung his wooden cane with the rounded crook. He used it when he was walking, because a long time ago he had hurt his left leg in an accident at the saw mill.

In the pews all around them were Grandpa and Grandma's other children and grandchildren, and some of their brothers and sisters. It was easy to tell which were Grandpa's brothers when they stood up, because they towered over all the people sitting around them. Daddy was big and tall, but Grandpa and his brothers were even taller—like giants. There were so many relatives that they filled up one whole side of the church.

"Do I have *so* many uncles and aunts and cousins?" asked Anna Rose. She knew them all because they came to the farm sometimes for Sunday visits. Usually only one or two families came at a time. She had never before seen them all together in one place.

"Ssshh!" whispered Mama. "Remember, you're in church."

Anna Rose listened carefully all through the Mass. Father Gara sang out the parts in his deep, resonant voice and the choir answered back. Occasionally, everyone in the church joined in the singing. When the Mass was over they got into the car again but instead of driving home Daddy slowed the car and turned in at Aunt Sophie and Uncle Roman's farm. They lived in the stone house that Grandpa had built when he married Grandma. Grandma and Grandpa still lived there, and Aunt Sophie took care of them.

"You sit quietly in the front room with your cousins," Mama told the middle girls as soon as they entered the house. "I'll be in the kitchen. Angeline, you put Virginia on the bed in Sophie's room and then come and help me peel potatoes."

Grandpa was already sitting in his rocking chair in the front room where he sat most of the winter. In spring he moved the rocker out to the front porch so he could look out over the main road to see who was going by.

Anna Rose perched on the edge of the sofa, next to her sisters. She dreaded what she knew would happen next. Sure enough, Grandpa beckoned to Millie. She walked over to him and he sat her on his right knee.

"Are you one of Alex's girls?" asked Grandpa in Polish. Mama had once explained that Grandpa always asked this because he had so many grandchildren, he couldn't keep them straight.

Millie nodded her head to say "Yes."

"Are you a good girl?" Grandpa continued.

Again, Millie nodded.

Grandpa asked her more questions in Polish, and Millie shook her head "Yes" or "No" to answer him. Then he let her go and motioned to Anna Rose. With trembling knees, she walked to Grandpa. He lifted her to his right knee.

"Can you understand me when I talk Polish?" Grandpa asked her, speaking in Polish.

Anna Rose was too scared to say anything, so she just nodded her head, copying Millie.

"Has the cat got your tongue?" Grandpa wanted to know. She hung her head. Why did grown-ups always ask that? Just because she was scared and shy didn't mean she couldn't talk! Grandpa asked her a few more questions in Polish and then he slid her off his knee. She scuttled back to the sofa.

Now it was Janie's turn. She wasn't shy at all. She jumped right up on Grandpa's knee and reached to touch his mustache. It hung down on both sides of his mouth, as far as his jaws.

"You have long whiskers," said Janie.

"Well, the cat hasn't got *your* tongue!" Grandpa

laughed. He wanted to know if she was a good girl and could say her prayers. He started her off on the "Our Father" in Polish and Janie said it right to the end. Grandpa patted her on the back.

Anna Rose was jealous. "It's not fair," she said to herself. "Everyone pays attention to Janie because she's got such pretty red curls. I could have said the 'Our Father' just as good as she did."

Anna Rose felt like pushing or shoving her sister, and she might have done it, only at that moment, Aunt Laura and Uncle John arrived with their children. They couldn't visit too often, because they lived in Winona and the trip to Grandpa's took almost an hour.

The cousins began laughing and chattering to each other in English. After dinner, they would go out together and play in the snow. Anna Rose put her arm around her cousin Laura, who was just the same age she was.

John and Jim were the oldest in that family. They were as tall as Lawrence, maybe even taller. They wanted to sneak away and join the other boys and men out in the barn, but Grandpa wasn't going to let them. He crooked his cane around Jim's neck and pulled him over to the rocker.

"Can't you talk in Polish?" scolded Grandpa.

All the children stopped talking.

"It's all right to talk English in school and in the stores," Grandpa lectured Jim, "but at home you should talk Polish. That's why your great-grandpa came here to America. So you'd have the right to talk Polish."

"Yes, Grandpa," said Jim meekly, in Polish. He unhooked his neck from the cane and edged toward the door. He wanted to be treated like a young man, not a little boy. But he didn't talk back to Grandpa.

Grandpa began to call the other children, one by one. Anna Rose slipped out to the kitchen. Mama and Aunt Sophie and Aunt Laura were chatting to each other in Polish as they prepared the dinner. In another corner, Daddy and Uncle Roman and Uncle John were discussing different things in the news. They were also talking in Polish.

"Why, they must have to obey Grandpa just like we have to obey Mama and Daddy!" Anna Rose found that idea a surprise. She had never noticed it before, but now she realized that Mama and Daddy spoke only in Polish when they were with Grandpa. At home, they sometimes used English and sometimes Polish.

"Go and see if Virginia is awake," Mama called to Anna Rose. "I think I hear her crying."

For the rest of the morning, Anna Rose and Millie and their cousins were busy running errands and setting the table. Every few minutes, it seemed, another uncle and aunt and more cousins arrived. A few of them could not stay long, so they just wished Grandpa a happy anniversary and quietly tiptoed into Grandma's room to pay their respects. Last of all came Uncle Albert and Aunt Stella and their children, who lived on the farm across the road.

Now there were more than fifty people who wanted to eat dinner. Not everyone could eat at once so they had to take turns. After each sitting, the dishes had to be washed and dried so the table could be set for the next group. At last, Anna Rose had her turn with Lawrence and Francis and some of their cousins. They ate all they could of the Polish sausage and baked ham, the potatoes and sauerkraut, the baked beans and green beans. After that, there was apple pie and poppy seed cake. The apple pie looked tasty, but Anna Rose could only manage one piece of poppy seed cake. The crunchy top and moist filling melted and joined in her mouth, tasting of honey and poppy seeds.

"Ma, how come your cake never turns out like this?" asked Lawrence in a teasing voice.

Mama laughed. She wasn't angry at all.

"I guess I'll leave it to Aunt Amelia and Aunt Sophie. I never could top them at making poppy seed cake."

When the meal was done and all the dishes washed and put away, some of the uncles and aunts started a game of cards called Sheepshead. Anna Rose wanted to watch so she could learn how to play. Her eyes followed the hands of the players as each lifted a card and slapped it neatly toward the center of the table. Every now and then, one of her uncles put down a card with a big thump.

"Here comes the boss!" he would say, as he put down the queen of clubs.

"So you had the Old One!" the others would exclaim. That was what they called the queen of clubs.

Angie and Millie and the cousins were dressing up in their snowsuits to go outside. Reluctantly, Anna Rose left the card game and went to put on her snowpants and galoshes. She hated her snowpants because they were tight and scratchy. Mama had made them out of an old, cast-off winter coat that someone had given her. The wool was so prickly, Anna Rose could feel it on her skin, even through her thick stockings and long underwear. She had to tuck her skirt into the top of the pants, and that made her feel as though she couldn't move.

"Why can't I have a snowsuit like Laura?" asked Anna Rose. Mama wasn't there to hear her, but Aunt Laura was.

"Shame on you, Anna Rose!" cried Aunt Laura. "You

should be glad your Mama can make you things to keep warm." Anna Rose knew Aunt Laura was right, but still, she didn't think it was fair that she always had to wear handed-down or made-over clothes. Laura's snowsuit was of soft blue wool and it didn't prick at all.

Anna Rose put on her heavy coat and Aunt Laura helped her to wind her scarf around and around her head and tie the ends in back. She put her mittens on and went out to join the others.

They were sledding down a gentle hill in front of the house. It was a perfect spot because they could go down in a curve and come around all the way to the bottom of the front driveway, ending up by the barn. It made a half-circle and that way they didn't have far to walk back. Two of the sleds were bobsleds that could hold four persons each. The third sled was small, so only two could go down on it. This meant they each had to wait their turn and could go down only every third time.

Francis sat down at the front of one of the bobsleds. He was going to steer, and Laura, Millie, and Anna Rose would hang on behind.

"I can go faster and further than you!" challenged their other cousin Jim. He was from Uncle Felix and Aunt Amelia's family.

"Okay, then, let's go." Both bobsleds lined up and they were given a shove by those waiting their turn.

Wheeee! Down and around the curve they raced, side by side.

"Lean to the right!" yelled Francis. Then: "Lean to the left!" He wanted them to take the curve smoothly, so they could get up speed and move ahead of the other sled.

Whiz! They passed Jim and the others and took the long turn toward the barn, finally coming to a stop in a snowbank. Jim's bobsled slid by and came to a stop a short distance ahead of them.

"We were faster!" bragged Francis.

"But we went further!" boasted Jim, and everyone laughed.

After that, they took different turns, with two of the older cousins always steering the sleds, and racing to see who could go fastest and furthest. Anna Rose didn't care who won. She wanted only the feeling of flying down in a

blur, faster than the wind. As she watched one group go down, she suddenly realized she had to go to the toilet.

"Oh, no!" she said to herself. "If I go in now I'll miss my turn!" She began to dance up and down in the snow. Angie was standing next to her.

"Do you have to go to the toilet?" asked Angie suspiciously. "If you do, you'd better go right now."

"I can wait until after my turn," Anna Rose assured her. "I'm next." But as the group trudged up the hill, she was not so sure.

"Hurry, hurry!" she called to them, jumping up and down. At last they reached the top of the hill. Anna Rose took her place on the sled. Jim was steering, and Angie and Sally Ann were sitting in front of her.

"One, two, three, go!" yelled Lawrence as he gave them a shove.

Down the hill flew the two sleds. But suddenly Anna Rose knew that she couldn't wait any longer.

"Stop! Stop!" she cried. Jim was too busy steering to hear her. Soon it was too late.

This time it was no fun flying down the hill with the wind whistling in her ears.

"I feel something wet," yelled Sally Ann. Behind her, Anna Rose started to cry. By the time they got to the bottom of the hill, she was sobbing.

"I told you to go in before we came down," said Angie softly, with pity in her voice.

"What's the matter?" asked Jim. Then he saw the big splotch of wetness running down Anna Rose's snow-pants. Sally Ann's pants had a few wet spots in back.

"Wet your pants, did you?" Jim said with a laugh. "Well, it happens to the best of us." He put his hand on Anna Rose's back as though to console her.

Anna Rose sobbed all the harder, burying her face in Angie's coat. The team from the other sled came up, wanting to know what happened. Anna Rose wouldn't look up at them. Still hiding behind Angie, and sobbing all the way, she followed the group up the hill.

"It's not a tragedy. Just an accident. No need to cry so hard," Mama said when Anna Rose came inside with the tears still streaming down her face.

"Now . . . the . . . others . . . will . . . make . . . fun . . . of . . . me!" Anna Rose blubbered.

"No, they won't," assured Mama. "It could happen to any one of them, and they know it. They won't tease you."

But Anna Rose knew better. She would never live this down, of that she was sure.

"Well, it's time to go home and do chores, so you won't be here for anyone to make fun of you," Mama spoke with finality. She called to Daddy and they bundled up Virgie and Mary Elizabeth and Janie and then hastily said their goodbyes.

They climbed into the car. Anna Rose sat in front this time, next to Mama. She was still wet and smelly, because there had been no other clothes for her to change into. To get to their farm, they had only to go over the hill, and down toward the river. It took about ten minutes, and all the while no one in the car spoke or made a noise.

"Maybe Mama was right," thought Anna Rose. Perhaps the others are just glad it didn't happen to them. Maybe they would not laugh at her after all. She hoped that was how it would be.

29

The Gander Bites

After the anniversary, Mama had to start doing all her own chores again. When the morning milking was done, Lawrence, Francis, Angie, and Millie went off to school in the buggy.

"I want to go to school, too," begged Anna Rose.

"You have to wait until you're old enough," said Mama with a sigh.

"How come Laura can go to kindergarten? I'm as old as she is," insisted Anna Rose.

"They don't have kindergarten at the school in Pine Creek," answered Mama. "But if you really want to go, I suppose you could live in Winona with Uncle John and Aunt Laura, like Francis did."

Anna Rose was silent. She wanted very badly to go to school, but she didn't want to leave her family. So she stayed at home and helped Mama with the work, or played with her younger sisters.

After breakfast, while Daddy cleaned the barn or did other work, Mama went to the cellar and separated the cream from the milk. Usually Anna Rose, Janie, and Mary Elizabeth went with her, while Virgie slept. They had to walk outside and around to the back of the house to get to their cellar. It had two flat doors, sloping down from the side of the house and out toward the backyard. The doors were covered with slippery metal and in spring and summer they could slide down them as though they were in a playground.

Now it was winter and the doors had a thin covering of ice and snow. Sometimes Mama had to chop through it with a small hatchet, in order to get the doors to lift up and open out.

The front cellar room was the separating room. The walls were of thick stone and the floor was concrete. Along one side was a built-in trough. It was partly filled with water and there was a constant trickle of more water coming out from a pipe at one side. In winter and in summer the water was icy cold because it came from a spring deep underground. In the water in the trough they kept the cans of cream that Daddy took to the creamery twice a week.

Jutting out into the room from one wall was the shiny black separating machine, with its long-handled crank hanging down at one side. At the top was a wide, round bowl. Into this, Mama poured the milk. She began to turn the crank at a steady pace.

"I want to turn it," said Anna Rose one morning.

"Well, then, you have to count as you turn it. You must make it go around thirty times in one minute. If you go like this: One . . . two . . . three . . . four . . . five . . .," Mama counted slowly, "that will make the right speed. Can you count up to thirty?"

Anna Rose turned the crank and counted slowly out loud, from one to thirty, with a pause between each number. When the crank was going smoothly, Mama turned the small handle of a spigot at the bottom of the bowl. Now it was harder to turn at the same speed. Before long, separate streams of cream and skim milk began to flow out. The cream went into a tall can and the milk dropped into the larger milk can. But it wasn't long before Anna Rose's arms got tired and Mama had to turn the crank once more.

When the skim milk and cream were separated, Mama took off the top bowl, pulled out the rod with the steel disks, and washed everything in hot soapy water. From a kettle, she poured boiling water over the bowl and disks, so that they would dry quickly and be free of germs.

All through February and March, Mama and the three girls started out their mornings down in the separating room of the cellar. Afterward, Mama had to do all her other work. Twice a week she wheeled out the washing machine to wash the diapers and other clothes. Virgie made a lot of diapers dirty. They didn't have electricity on their farm, so the washing machine had to run on a gasoline motor. It made a lot of rackety noise.

Three times a week Mama baked bread. She would let the dough rise, punch it down, then let it rise again. Finally, she would shape it into eight fat loaves and put each into a pan. Once more the dough had to rise and at last the loaves were ready to go into the oven. After an hour, Mama took them out, crispy and golden brown. Somehow, the bread always got done about a half-hour before the older children came home from school. They wanted to eat some before starting their chores.

"I get the crust!" yelled Lawrence.

"No fair! You had it last time," argued Angie. They each wanted the end piece because it was so crunchy and tasty. When the bread was a day or more old, they didn't argue so much over the end crust, but when it was fresh out of the oven, Mama made them take turns cutting off the first slice.

Saturday bread baking was the best. Before the dough got kneaded into a round, satiny ball, Mama took part of it and put it into another large bowl. She added sugar and raisins and a little milk and more flour before she kneaded it and set it to rise, next to the big bowl of bread dough.

"Punch the bread down for me, Angeline," Mama would say if she was busy doing something else. Angie would rub her hands with a light coating of lard and punch down the bread dough and the sweet dough. She had learned how to knead it with the palms of her hands and how to turn it over again so it made a smooth, round shape.

"Can't I do that?" asked Anna Rose. She thought it would be fun, and it looked easy.

"You have to watch for a long time, and then practice a lot before you get it just right," said Mama. "Pretty soon I'll let you try with your own little loaf."

After the bread loaves were shaped, Mama took her rolling pin and rolled out the sweet dough in two big rectangles. Over these she spread more raisins, and sugar and cinnamon. Then she folded over one long edge of the rectangle and began to curl it up, as though it were a small carpet being rolled up. She cut the plump coil into slices, lined them up on baking sheets, almost touching each other, and brushed them with butter. The sheets were set aside for the dough to rise once more, but not as long as the dough for the bread loaves. Finally, into the oven they went, and when they came out they were covered with fat, puffy coils of golden brown. Here and there a raisin had popped out, making a splotch of dark brown.

Mama called them snails, because they looked like the coiled shell of a snail. As soon as they cooled off for a few minutes, she slathered vanilla frosting over the tops, so much that it dripped down the sides. One batch they saved to eat for breakfast on Sunday, but the other they could eat on Saturday afternoon, after all the cleaning and chores were done. They sighed with satisfaction, gulping down mugs of cold milk in between bites of sweet snails.

In early April, Mama was busier than ever. In one corner of the garden she planted the first rows of lettuce, onions, and radishes.

"I don't care if I am taking a risk that a hard frost will kill them," she said. "I'm so hungry for fresh vegetables that I can't wait."

The weather stayed mild, and in two weeks there were rows of tiny green shoots in the garden. The grass and hay started coming up, too, and that meant the geese and gander could be let out of the shed where they spent the winter. Every day after school, Angie and Millie had to go looking for the secret hiding places where the geese chose to lay their eggs.

"Those darn geese," complained Angie. "Why can't they lay their eggs where they are supposed to?" Then she had an idea. "Anna Rose, can you watch out during the day, and tell me where the geese go? Then I'll know where to look for the eggs. But don't get too near that gander. He's a mean one and he'll bite you."

Every day after that, while Mama worked in the garden and Janie and Mary Elizabeth puddled around making mud pies, Anna Rose tried to watch carefully where the geese went. She never walked too close behind them because as soon as she came within a few yards of them, Hissssssss!, the gander would turn toward her, neck stretched out and beak wide open, ready to bite. Anna Rose ran as fast as she could, to the safety of the house or the garden. In the late afternoon, she told Angie where to look for the eggs.

Soon, there were three broody hens and two geese sitting on nests of eggs. Mama made a mark on the calendar hanging on the kitchen wall.

"We have to watch carefully after thirty days to see that the eggs hatch out all right. We should have about forty goslings, if we're lucky." Mama was happy about that.

Angie still had to watch out for the geese in the afternoon, spreading mash in their feeders and making sure there was enough water in their trough. The gander hissed a bit when she did that, but it was just for show. He didn't come after her.

On May 20th, when she went to give the geese their usual food, Angie heard a funny "Whit, whit!" Sticking out from one of the nests was the head of a gosling. Back she ran to the house.

"They're starting to hatch!" she said excitedly to Anna Rose. Then she turned to Mama. "Should I make some of the special mash?"

"Yes," answered Mama. "Bring some skim milk from

the cellar and I'll show you how to mix it with the mash."
They stirred the mixture until it was like a thick porridge.
After spreading it in small, low pans, Angie returned to
the nests where the goslings were hatching. She poked
the beak of a gosling into the mash and then into the
water. Soon, the gosling knew how to eat by itself.

Within seven days, all the eggs were hatched but one.

"It's probably rotten and won't hatch out," Mama
explained. "You'll have to throw it away, Angeline. Take
it out from the nest when the goose isn't looking and
throw it far down in the big ditch, where we can't smell
it."

Anna Rose watched as Angie skillfully sneaked the
egg away when the geese and gander were busy gobbling
up mash. Gingerly, she carried the large egg in her
cupped hands, all the way to the big ditch, where she
threw it down as far as she could. Plock! The egg landed
far down, but even so, the smell began to rise up in
penetrating fumes.

"Phew! Let's get out of here," cried Angie, holding
her nose.

By the end of May when school was out for the
summer, the goslings were covered with a soft, white
down.

"Now you have to start feeding them nettles," Mama
told Angie and Millie. "Remember to chop them up fine,
like I showed you last year. Anna Rose can help you pick
the leaves. It's time she started learning how."

Angie and Millie both groaned. That was just about
the worst job they could think of. Nettles had something
on their leaves that made your skin itch. They called the
nettles by their Polish name, which sounded like *pok-shee-vas*.

"That makes me think of something that pokes and

36

prickles," thought Anna Rose, and that was what the leaves seemed to do.

"Why do we have to cut up those *pok-shee-vas* for the geese?" she asked. "Can't they eat them off the plants where they are growing?"

"The big geese can do that because they have strong beaks, but the goslings can't tear or chew for a while yet, so we have to cut things up for them," explained Mama. "Goslings need to eat green things to grow; *pok-shee-vas* happen to have a flavor that geese like. My grandma once told me that in Poland they used to boil up the young *pok-shee-vas* and eat them as vegetables, so they must be tasty. Shall I make some for supper?" asked Mama with a laugh.

"Ugh! I would never in my life eat boiled *pok-shee-vas*," said Millie in a disgusted voice. Anna Rose firmly shook her head "No" and closed her mouth tight. No one would *ever* get her to eat such a thing! Nettles were quite different from Brown Betty. She didn't have to see them cooked to know she would not like them.

"I'm only teasing," said Mama. "I'm not going to boil any *pok-shee-vas*." But they still had to pick them every day for Angie to chop up. If they put on their mittens, they couldn't tear off the leaves properly. When they used old cloth gloves or wrapped their hands in a dishcloth, the nettles still stung their skin, right through the cloth. There was nothing to do except pick them as fast as they could, then run into the house and wash their hands and arms with lots of soap and water. That seemed to stop the stinging.

One morning Mama announced that she and Daddy had to go to Winona on some business.

"I think this time Angeline and Mildred may go along. They have not had a turn for quite a while," said

Mama. "That means you have to take care of the little ones, Francis, and you'll have to do all the barn work by yourself, Lawrence."

"Gee whiz," complained Francis. "Can't one of them stay home?" He had had to take care of Millie when she was little, but now that she and Angie were old enough, he didn't see why he should have to take his turn again. "Besides, I don't know how to change diapers any more," Francis stated flatly, sure that this excuse would be a good one.

"You won't have to. I'll take Virginia with me because she is still nursing, and she's no trouble. She sleeps most of the time. You only have to watch out for Mary Elizabeth and Jane and Anna Rose. Weed at least ten rows of potatoes in the garden and be sure to do the *pok-shee-vas* for the geese."

"And watch out that the gander doesn't get near the girls," added Daddy. "He's been acting so fierce of late, he'll bite anyone who comes his way."

Lawrence ducked out of the house and headed for the barn as fast as he could. He didn't want to be given any extra jobs. All morning, Francis grumbled but he stayed close to the house, watching his sisters.

"Aren't you going to feed the geese?" asked Anna Rose, when it was almost time to eat. She wanted to see how he did it.

"I'm going to wait until Mary Elizabeth takes her nap. Then she won't be following me around," Francis replied.

Mama had left some sausage meat on the table, and there were eggs in a bowl that Francis had to scramble and cook on the stove. He sliced a loaf of bread, and buttered a slice for each of his sisters. There was also a quart jar of raspberries that Mama had left as a special treat. Lawrence opened it and spooned the red berries and juice into five bowls. He gave himself and Francis the most, but they all had second helpings. Soon the whole jar was empty.

After they had put the dishes in the sink, Lawrence went out to the machine shed to hitch up the cultivator, and Francis put Mary Elizabeth on the small cot in the spare bedroom off the front room. That was where she always took her nap.

They went out to the potato patch above the garden where row after row of new plants were struggling to hold their own against the weeds. Francis showed the two girls how to grab hold of the crabgrass and weeds close to the ground and pull hard without tearing out any of the potato plants. Janie started on the first row, but before long she was playing in the dirt, forgetting all about the weeds. Anna Rose worked slowly and methodically on her row.

"She should weed, too," protested Anna Rose.

"Let her be," answered Francis. "She would pull up too many plants anyway."

They weeded for more than an hour. It was hot and Anna Rose was tired of leaning over and stooping down. There were still so many rows left to do.

"Let's stop," she pleaded. "Isn't it time to feed the geese?"

"All right," agreed Francis. He was tired of weeding, too.

"I'll help you pick the *pok-shee-vas*," offered Anna Rose.

Carrying a big pan, they set off for the back part of the orchard where many nettles grew in clumps. Janie followed them, clutching two fistfuls of dirt. As fast as they could, Francis and Anna Rose plucked leaves from the stinging plants until the pan was full.

"That should be enough," said Francis. Anna Rose

tore back to the house and washed her arms and hands in soap and water. When she came outside again, Francis was already chopping up the nettles, using a long, sharp knife and a flat board. Janie watched for a while and then wandered off. Just then, they heard Mary Elizabeth crying and calling out.

"Go and get her up," Francis ordered Anna Rose. She went into the house and back to the spare room. Mary Elizabeth stopped crying the moment she saw her.

"Drink!" she demanded.

Anna Rose took her by the hand and led her to the kitchen sink. She ran water into a glass and gave it to Mary Elizabeth. Above the sink and just off to the side was a big window that looked out on the backyard and orchard. Standing on the little stool, Anna Rose could see Francis, chop-chopping at the nettles. Behind him a few yards to the right was Janie. She was stretching out her hands to one of the goslings that had wandered away from the rest. It must have smelled the nettles, and was coming to get some to eat. Closer and closer came the gosling. Janie reached down to catch it so she could pet it.

All of a sudden, Anna Rose gasped. There, half flying across the backyard, was the mean gander, headed straight for Janie! Janie couldn't see the gander coming because she was bent down over the gosling. Francis had his back turned as he busily chopped the nettles.

"Stop him!" shrieked Anna Rose, but, of course, Francis could not hear. She reached for a spoon to bang on the window and just as she did, Francis looked up and saw the gander.

Too late! The gander had snapped his beak right into Janie's bottom.

"Ow! Ow! Ow!" howled Janie.

"Get away from here!" yelled Francis as he swatted

the knife and board at the gander, sending the chopped nettles flying in all directions. The gander let go of Janie. Francis dropped the knife and board, picked her up and ran with her into the house. Janie was sobbing and screaming.

Francis sat down on a chair and lay Janie across his knees, on her stomach. He lifted up her dress and pushed aside her panties. There, on one of Janie's buttocks, was a big round bite mark, all red and swollen and bleeding a little. The two girls stared at it while Janie continued to cry.

"Ow! Ow! Ow!"

Francis took her to the front room and laid her on the couch. Anna Rose and Mary Elizabeth followed silently.

"Watch her for a minute," Francis said in a shaky voice. He went back to the sink, rinsed out a clean cloth in cold water, and took the small bottle of iodine from the medicine chest. Gently he washed the gander bite and held the cold cloth against the wound. Janie only whimpered now.

"I'm going to put some iodine on it. It will sting for a while but then it will feel better," Francis assured Janie, but Anna Rose could see he looked scared. Would Janie get sick from the gander bite? She had heard of people getting sick or dying from a dog bite. That was why Mama told them to stay away from any strange dogs that wandered on to the farm by accident.

"Hold on to her legs," whispered Francis. Anna Rose grabbed hold of Janie's feet. As fast as he could, Francis swabbed the iodine over the bite mark, but still Janie screamed.

"It pinches! It pinches!" Janie kicked her legs so hard she almost hit Anna Rose in the jaw. At last she calmed down and lay still.

"You stay with her while I go finish feeding the geese and start my other chores," said Francis.

Janie lay quietly and Anna Rose took out one of the reading books from the shelf. She pretended to read it aloud. She knew a lot of the pages by heart because Angie had read them to her so many times. "If I could only go to school, then I'd really know how to read," thought Anna Rose.

The dogs began to bark. Anna Rose ran to the front porch.

"Mama and Daddy are back!"

Janie slid off the couch and ran out of the house toward her mother, who was just getting out of the car.

"Mama, Mama!" she cried. "The gander bit me in the *dupa!*"

Anna Rose gasped. *Dupa* was a naughty word in Polish. They weren't supposed to use it at all.

Mama didn't know what to say or do. She looked as though she wanted to laugh and scold at the same time. Without a word, she put her arm around Janie, and then examined the gander bite.

"I thought you were supposed to be minding the girls," Daddy scolded Francis angrily.

"I *was* minding them," protested Francis, trying to explain.

"If you had been paying attention, Janie would not have got bitten. Bring me my strap from the kitchen. If you can't learn to mind when we tell you to do something, then I'll have to teach you another way!" Daddy's voice was hard and angry.

Francis hung his head and went to the kitchen for the razor strap. Daddy took him behind the woodpile.

Whack! Whack! Whack! They heard three loud smacks.

Anna Rose felt sorry for Francis. It was not his fault that the gander came up so suddenly. Janie shouldn't have been playing with the gosling anyway.

That night, at the supper table, Janie sat on a soft feather pillow because her bottom still hurt if she sat on something hard.

"Let that be a lesson to all of you," Mama spoke seriously. "You have to learn to obey, or you'll get hurt."

When Francis came in, he sat down slowly and stiffly.

"Does your *dupa* hurt, too?" Janie asked him.

Everyone at the table started laughing, even Francis and Daddy.

"Don't you be saying words like that. It's not nice," Mama scolded Janie, but they could see she was holding back a laugh.

43

The Broken Toe

"Oh, no! There's that old sow in the garden again," moaned Angie as she passed by the kitchen window. "Come on, Millie and Anna Rose. You have to help me get her back in the pen."

They went out the side door and up to the vegetable garden. The sow was rooting up the new lettuce plants and gobbling them up as fast as she could. Angie circled around the back and Millie and Anna Rose stayed in front, to prevent the sow from going into the cabbages and the hillocks of cucumber vines that were just beginning to spread out in creeping tendrils. Mama worked so hard getting them planted and weeded that they knew she would be angry if the sow got into that part of the garden.

"Shoo, shoo!" cried Angie, giving the sow a prod with a twig that she picked up. The sow grunted and kept on eating.

"Run and get a good, strong stick," Angie called to Anna Rose.

Anna Rose went to the summer kitchen, where Mama always kept her mops and pails. She remembered that there was an old mop stick there, with no mop on it. It was thick and round and sturdy.

"Here," Anna Rose handed it to Angie, carefully staying as far away from the sow as she could.

Whack! Angie thumped the sow on her rump. She stopped rooting up lettuces and moved toward the upper part of the garden, where the potato patch was. The girls moved behind her, guiding her toward the corner that was nearest to the pigpen.

Suddenly, the sow turned and ran back toward the cabbages and cucumbers and started munching on the succulent young cabbage leaves.

"Run and get Ma," called Angie. "We'll never get her back in by ourselves."

"Mama, we can't get that sow back into her pen. She's eating your cabbages," Anna Rose informed her mother, panting to catch her breath. That was all Mama needed to hear. She went out to the garden in a hurry, taking with her a small pail of garbage from the kitchen.

"Pooik, pooik, pooik," Mama yodeled as she moved close enough for the sow to smell the potato peelings and leftover oatmeal in the pail. The sow lifted up her head and started to follow Mama, grunting with every step. At last, they came close to the pigpen. There, under one part of the fence, was a big space that the sow had dug out.

Mama lifted one of the boards higher and put the pail on the ground inside the pen. The sow didn't want to go back in. She turned around, looking as though she wanted to bolt back to the lettuce and cabbages.

"Get in there, you ornery critter," yelled Mama as she snatched the stick from Angie's hands and gave the sow a swat on the rear end. With a squeal, the sow went back into the pen.

"We have to find something to put here or she will go right back into the garden," said Mama. "Run and get me that big ax from the woodshed, and some wooden stakes."

Angie found the ax and Anna Rose and Millie each carried an armload of wooden stakes up to the pigpen fence where Mama waited. First, Mama chopped one end of each stake with the ax, until it was pointy. Then, with the broad side of the ax she pounded in the stakes, one by one, making a sturdy fence alongside the fence that was already there.

"That ought to do the trick," Mama said with a satisfied look.

But it didn't. Twice more in the next week the old sow managed to sneak back into the garden. Somehow, she could always poke and push with her snout until she had made a hole big enough to go through. Mama's cabbages and cucumbers were beginning to look scrawny and trampled.

"Alex," said Mama one day to their father. "You are going to have to do something about that sow, or sell her. I can't have her ruining my garden."

"*Sell* her?" Daddy asked in astonishment. "I can't do that. She's one of the best sows we have and always gives a good litter."

"I don't care," replied Mama. "Either you fix that fence so she can't get through, or get rid of her." Mama was determined not to let the sow get into the garden one more time. She worked hard, weeding and hoeing and hilling, until all the rows of vegetables were neat and orderly. The girls had to help almost every day, and they didn't want the sow to mess up their work, either.

The next day, Daddy and Lawrence took a wheelbarrow full of newly sawed planks, some posts, and the post hole digger out to the pigpen.

"We'll make a brand-new fence," said Daddy. "She surely can't get through that." Anna Rose watched as he and Lawrence took turns, lifting up the post hole digger and bringing it down with a thud. They pushed the handles apart, and that held in the dirt between the two blades, like a giant pincher. Again and again they thumped the digger into the ground and lifted up the dirt, until they had a deep hole. Then they started the next hole a few feet away. Soon there was a row of holes. Into each one they put a post and stamped the earth tight around the part where the post stuck up above the ground. Finally, they fastened the boards from post to post, and braced them with cross pieces. When they were finished, the new fence shone white in the sun, straight and sturdy.

"There, you old sow, just try getting under that," challenged Lawrence as he gave a last pound with the mallet on top of each post, making sure they were deep in the ground.

For a week, nothing happened. The sow stayed in her pen and the girls helped their mother in the garden. The cucumbers and cabbages began to look full and leafy again.

But one morning, when Anna Rose went to the woodpile to get an armload of wood for the kitchen stove, she glanced at the garden and there, rooting about in the cabbages, was the old sow. She threw down the wood and raced into the house.

"Mama, Mama!" she shrieked. "That sow is in the garden again!"

"I don't believe it!" cried Mama, but all the same she went to the door to have a look. Her face became hard and set.

"Angeline, Mildred, all you girls! Get out there and chase her back toward the pen. I'm going to see how she managed to get out." Mama walked up to the new fence. There, in a corner where it connected to a piece of the old fence, the sow had dug and pushed until one of the posts leaned sideways, making a hole big enough for her to get through. Down through the potato patch marched Mama, looking angry and determined. The girls were trying to get the sow to move but it would not budge.

"Pooik, pooik, pooik," called their mother, but the sow paid no attention. Instead, it turned and ran toward the front yard. Anna Rose and Janie were supposed to be guarding that spot, but when the fat sow came running right at them, they got scared and jumped out of the way.

"Head her off!" yelled Angie to Millie, but it was already too late. The sow was now in the front yard, munching on the roots and stems of the peony bushes.

"Oh, no!" said Anna Rose. "Is Mama ever going to be mad!" The six peony bushes in the front yard were Mama's special flowers. Every year she nursed them carefully along, digging up the bulby roots and separating them when they got too big. In the spring, the bushes were covered with masses of pink blooms, spreading their fragrance through the front yard. Sometimes Mama took a bouquet to church, for the altar.

When Mama came walking back from the pigpen and saw the sow chomping on her peony bushes, she broke into a run and headed straight for the sow. She looked around for a moment, searching for a stick. When she saw

48

nothing handy, she gave the sow a good, strong kick in the rump.

"Damn you! Get out of my garden!" shouted Mama, as the sow went off squealing.

Anna Rose opened her eyes wide. Never had she heard her mother swear. They were taught never to use words like that.

As Angie and Millie and Janie came tearing into the front yard, there was Mama, leaning against the fence. She was holding one foot behind the other, and small tears were beginning to squeeze out of her eyes.

"Angeline, run and get your Pa and tell him to come right away. I think I broke my toe." Mama could hardly talk, the pain was so bad.

For some reason, Anna Rose wanted to laugh, but she knew she didn't dare. She could tell Mama was really mad from the way her eyelids fluttered and the way her mouth was held in a thin, straight line.

"Help me sit down on the front steps," Mama said to Millie and Anna Rose as she motioned them to come close. The girls stood on either side of her and, leaning heavily on their shoulders, she limped and half hopped to the front steps. There she sat down and gave a moan of pain.

"Take off my shoe as gently as you can," Mama pleaded.

Millie carefully unlaced the shoelace and slipped off Mama's right shoe. Mama winced and sucked in her breath. Then Millie took off her stocking. Anna Rose could see that her big toe was swollen and slanted to one side.

Daddy came running up, with Lawrence and Francis right behind. Before he could ask what had happened, Mama started talking, half sobbing as she spoke.

"Alex, I don't care what you say, you are taking that damn pig to market and selling her today! You can do it while I go to the doctor. Just look what that devil did to my toe."

Daddy was as shocked as the rest of them at the language Mama used. Without saying a word, he motioned to the children to help him corner the sow.

Then he called out to Angie.

"Bring me that rope that's hanging right inside the barn door."

As soon as Angie had brought the rope, Daddy and the boys caught the sow and tied up her legs, so she could hardly move. She squealed and grunted the whole time. Then, Daddy backed the truck up to the front yard gate, leaned a platform against it, like a ramp, and they pushed and prodded the sow up the boards until she was resting on the back of the truck. They put the sides on the truck and Lawrence spread some straw all around the sow. He untied the rope they had used, and went to hang it in the barn again.

While they were doing that, Mama went into the house, hobbling as best she could on one leg. She came out now, wearing one of her good dresses and carrying her purse. Anna Rose could see she was still sniffling a little. Without saying another word, Mama and Daddy both got in the truck and drove off. Lawrence came back from the barn and watched them depart.

"Damn pig! She hurt Mama's toe!" cried Janie.

Lawrence looked at Francis and they turned away, walking toward the toolshed. Anna Rose could see their shoulders shaking, as though they were laughing hard.

"You had better not let Mama hear you saying such a swear word. She would wash your mouth out with soap and water," Angie scolded Janie, but Anna Rose could see that she, too, was having a hard time keeping a straight face.

Later in the day, when the truck pulled into the yard, they could see that the sow was gone. Daddy helped Mama out of the truck and into the house. Her right big toe was wrapped with white adhesive tape, and along one side were taped some flat, thin sticks.

Mama came into the kitchen and the girls stood around her, looking serious and wide-eyed.

"Well," said Mama with an embarrassed laugh, "I guess I taught that old sow a lesson and she taught me one, too. Never kick a pig, unless you've got iron-toed boots."

Anna Rose thought Mama was going to say something else, but she didn't. Maybe she was ashamed of getting so mad and using those swear words.

Mama hobbled over to the sink and started the water running.

"Are you going to wash your mouth out with soap and water?" asked Anna Rose in shocked surprise.

Mama turned around with an astounded look. Then she laughed.

"I was only going to take a drink but I guess I should wash those bad words away." Lightly, she pretended to rub the soap back and forth over her tongue, making a funny face all the while. Then she took a long drink of water.

The girls giggled. Now the uneasy feelings were gone, and they could laugh at Mama. It didn't matter, because she was laughing at herself, too.

Chopping Thistles

"Those thistles are about to take over the oats on the upper forty," said Daddy at the dinner table one Monday in July. "Angie and Millie, you had better go out there this afternoon. Pull out the ones you can, by the roots. The rest you can chop out with a hoe. Try not to cut down any oats."

The upper forty and the lower forty were the two biggest fields on their farm. They were each forty acres. One was above the road and the other was below it.

Angie and Millie did not like being asked to do that job. It was hot in the oats field, and the thistles were prickly and hard to chop out. But they dared not complain because when Daddy gave orders like that, he meant that the work was important, and had to be done as soon as possible.

Right after they finished eating, Angie and Millie took a jar of water and set out for the field. They did not come in until suppertime, so Anna Rose had to carry wood from the stacked pile to the bin in the summer kitchen. When it was so hot, Mama didn't light the stove in the regular kitchen. Instead, she did all the cooking in a small shed at the side of the house, called the summer kitchen.

On Tuesday, the girls again took their bottles of water and walked out to the oats field to chop thistles. In the late afternoon Daddy went to see how many thistles were left, and they walked back together.

"How are the thistle choppers doing?" asked Mama as they sat down to supper.

"One more day should do it," answered Daddy. "They haven't missed many, so we should get a nice clean threshing of oats."

Angie and Millie smiled proudly. They were doing a good job. On Wednesday, without complaining and without being asked, they set off for the oats field. Anna Rose noticed that Angie had a bulge under the front of her shirt. She was going to ask about it when Angie ran up the road to the gate, leaving her behind.

On Thursday afternoon, after they had eaten, Angie sauntered out the kitchen door.

"I'm going to chop thistles," she called to Mama as she slammed the screen door.

"I thought you finished yesterday," said Mama.

"No, there are still some left, and I want to clear every last thistle from that field," yelled Angie as she moved toward the road. Then she added quickly: "Millie doesn't have to come. I can finish by myself." Angie walked swiftly, but stiffly, up to the gate, and then she turned left, out of sight.

"She was hiding something under her shirt again," Anna Rose said softly. "I wonder what it was." A few minutes later, when she went to the kitchen to get a drink, she saw two jars standing to one side of the sink.

"Mama, Angie forgot her water jar. Can I take her some water later?" asked Anna Rose.

Mama looked up from the rocker, where she was nursing Virgie.

"So, you want to go chop thistles, too!" laughed Mama. "All right, in a little while you can take her some water, but Mildred has to go with you, to show you the way."

At first, Millie did not want to go.

"It's too hot to walk that far for nothing," she protested. "Angie will come home as soon as she is thirsty."

"Just take her up to the edge of the field, so she can see where Angeline is working. You can come right back and she can walk the rest of the way by herself." Mama turned to Anna Rose: "You'll have to wait and walk home with Angeline. I don't want you getting lost. That's a big field and you could easily get turned around."

An hour later, Anna Rose let the water run until it was icy cold. She filled one of the jars and put on the cap.

"I'm ready," she called to Millie. They started up the incline that led to the big gate. On the other side of the gate was the road, and beyond that, the fields.

At first the jar felt good against her hands; it was so cool in the hot sun. But soon her fingers began to get a little numb.

"Can you carry it for a while?" she asked Millie. "I'm afraid I'll drop it."

"Oh, all right," said Millie. She had been hoping she could get to hold the cool jar against her hot, sticky arms. She held it first cradled in her right arm, then her left. They were walking along the road now and not too far ahead was the upper forty.

"That's funny. I can't see Angie anywhere in the field," said Millie, shading her eyes against the direct sun.

They walked right up to the edge of the field. Sloping gently upward before them, almost as far as Anna Rose could see, were row after row of golden yellow oats. At the head of each stalk were fronds of kernels, each in its own bearded husk. When she stood next to the stalks they came up to her chest.

Millie's eyes scanned the field in all directions. She saw no sign of Angie. Handing the water jar back to Anna Rose, she cupped her hands to her mouth and called as loudly as she could.

"Angie! Angie! Where are you?"

In answer, the only sounds they heard were the soft rustlings of the oat stalks as they brushed against each other. Millie called out once more.

"Angie!"

At the upper edge of the field stood a small group of poplar trees, near the head of a small ravine. Suddenly, they saw the light blue of Angie's shirt pop up under the trees. They saw her put her hands to her face, and heard a faint echo of her voice but could not make out what she said.

"You can go on now by yourself," Millie directed. "Just keep heading straight up to her."

Anna Rose pushed her way forward through the oats. Only her head and shoulders were visible. Millie turned and walked back on the road toward the gate.

From the top of the field Angie started walking toward Anna Rose. They met in the middle of the field.

"What are you doing here?" asked Angie.

"I brought you some water. You forgot it." Anna Rose held out the jar. It was no longer cool to the touch.

"Oh!" was all Angie said as she reached for the jar, unscrewed the cover, and took a long drink.

"That tasted good," she said. "But you didn't have to bring it. I could have waited until I got home." They stood there silently for a few moments. Angie didn't seem to know what to do. Finally Anna Rose spoke.

"Can I help you chop thistles?"

That helped Angie make up her mind.

"Okay. There are not many left. You try to pull up the small ones and I'll chop out the tall ones because I have only this one hoe. There is only that one spot, over there beyond the ravine, that hasn't been finished yet."

They walked down and up, to the other side of the ravine, and Angie showed Anna Rose how to grasp hard, with both hands, low down on the thistle plant, and pull with all her might. Sometimes the plant came up but other times she couldn't make it budge. Then Angie would cut the thistle with her shiny, sharp hoe. They piled the thistle plants between the rows of oats. Later, they would take them to the side of the road, so they would not get mixed up with the oats again, or seed themselves in the field.

The piles of thistles began to get higher and Anna Rose began to get hotter and thirstier. All the water in the jar was gone.

"Aren't we finished yet? I don't see any more thistles," Anna Rose complained in a tired, whiny voice.

"I see a few short plants here and there, but I don't think they will matter. Let's go home." Angie began to bind up the thistle piles into two bundles, using thin stalks as though they were rope. She turned up toward the poplar trees at the top of the field.

"How come you're going that way?" asked Anna Rose. "Can't we leave the thistles down by the road? We would be closer to home."

"I left something up by the trees," Angie explained.

Anna Rose did not say a word. Whatever it was, it must have been what Angie was carrying under her shirt when she left the house.

When they came nearer to the trees, Angie started walking faster, trying to get ahead of her sister. She dropped the bundle of thistles next to a pile that was already there, and ran to pick up something. Before she could get it hidden under her shirt, Anna Rose saw that it was a book.

"Were you reading up here?" she asked in surprise. Angie always seemed to have a book in her hands around the house, but Anna Rose wondered what she wanted with a book up here in the field. Then she knew. "You said you were going to chop thistles, and you were reading instead," she accused Angie.

"I *did* chop some thistles, can't you see?" protested Angie. "It's just that I'm always getting interrupted in the house. Here, it is so peaceful and quiet I can read five chapters without stopping. You won't tell anyone, will you?"

Anna Rose thought about it for a while. Angie really had chopped out some thistles. And she was good about reading aloud to them almost every night. Sometimes she told them made-up stories, and that was even better.

"No, I won't tell," she promised Angie.

They trudged home and when they got close to the house, Angie was careful to slip around to the front entrance while Anna Rose went to the summer kitchen to tell Mama about all the thistles they had pulled.

That night Angie read to her younger sisters, and told them another story about "The Adventures of Pal." Pal was their dog and he was an ordinary watchdog, but Angie could make up lots of exciting stories about him: how he once saved a girl from drowning; how he caught the robbers coming to steal something in the dead of night. She always told it as though the stories took place on their farm. For the spooky parts, her voice got low and whispery and slow. Anna Rose and Janie and Mary Elizabeth sat without moving, wondering what would happen next. Usually, at that point in the story, Angie would shout something, and the girls would jump and give a squeal or shriek. They loved being scared like that.

Tonight, Angie told how Pal rescued a girl named Anna. She had fainted on the railroad tracks, just before a train was supposed to come along. Angie's voice went lower and slower as she told the story:

In the distance, the train whistled. Anna did not hear it. She had fainted dead away, with her head across one of the rails. In the yard, Pal looked around. He did not see Anna. He heard the train whistle. Like a shot, he took off down the road that led to the railroad crossing. He came to a high gate. It was closed. Pal had never jumped over such a high gate. Only a horse could do it. The train was coming closer, closer, closer. Pal ran and leaped forward. The gate was too high. He could not even get near the top. Again and again Pal tried, each time jumping a little higher. Clo--ser, clo---ser, clo---ser came the train.

Angie's voice was now a soft, long-drawn-out whisper. Quietly, slowly, she put her hands to her mouth. Suddenly, she let out a piercing whistle: "Wheeeeeeee!"

Mary Elizabeth jumped and grabbed onto Angie. Janie pulled the sheet over her head. Anna Rose leaped out of bed.

"What happened?" she cried.

"When Pal heard that whistle so close," Angie continued, "he took one mighty leap, cleared the gate, ran to the tracks, caught hold of Anna by her dress and pulled her off the tracks—just as the train whizzed by. But he couldn't get his tail out of the way in time, so the tip was cut off by the train. And that's why Pal's tail has no tip."

Anna Rose breathed a sigh of relief. She knew it was a made-up story. Pal would never be able to do something like that. But Angie made it seem so real that while she was telling it, Anna Rose was sure it could happen.

"I'll never tell about what you do when you go chopping thistles," she whispered in Angie's ear.

Sounding Out
"Cin-na-mon"

Crack! Boom! Swish! The lightning, thunder, and rain of an early August storm flashed and rolled, filling the farmyard with noise. Anna Rose was in the house with her mother and sisters, waiting out the storm. It was not the dangerous kind of storm that might turn into a tornado. Daddy and the boys were in the barn, getting ready to whitewash the walls and ceiling.

Mama had lighted the candles and said a prayer, but she was not pacing nervously back and forth, as she sometimes did when a really bad storm came along. She punched down the bread dough for the last time and divided it into eight loaves. After setting them off to one side of the stove to rise, she went back to her sewing.

On the couch in the front room, Millie and Janie were playing with paper dolls. Angie sat by herself, reading a mystery book. She had read it many times before, but whenever a rainy day came along, and they couldn't work or play outside, she reread one of her favorite books. Anna Rose wanted to read those books, too. When she opened them, she saw they were full of long, hard words. One of the books on the shelf was called *More Dick and Jane Stories* and it had short, easy words. Anna Rose knew most of them by heart because Angie had read it aloud so many times. But when she tried to find those same words in the fat books, they did not seem to be there. If only she could go to school! Then she would learn all the big words in every book. That gave her an idea.

"Let's play school, so you can teach us more words," Anna Rose suggested to Angie.

"Play school," echoed Mary Elizabeth. She toddled over to where Anna Rose was trying to get Angie's attention.

"Don't bother me now. I'm just at an exciting part." Angie motioned them away.

"Read *that* book to us," Anna Rose pleaded.

"Read us," imitated Mary Elizabeth.

"You wouldn't understand it. You have to know the story from the start. Besides, there are too many hard words. I can hardly pronounce some of them." Angie dismissed them with a firm look and buried her face in the book again.

Anna Rose was sure she would be able to understand. That was the trouble with older sisters. Sometimes they told you things and other times it was as if they purposely decided to keep what they knew a secret, so they could act smarter than you.

"There is nothing to do around here," complained Anna Rose.

"How can you say that?" protested Mama. "You have your deck of cards and your coloring book and crayons. And what about the Uncle Wiggily game? You could play that."

Anna Rose brightened up. Mary Elizabeth was too young to play the Uncle Wiggily game. She always wanted to move the markers when it was not her turn. But maybe Millie and Janie would play. She went over to them.

"Will you play Uncle Wiggily with me?"

"No, we want to finish this first," insisted Millie.

"Nobody wants to play with me," grumbled Anna Rose.

"How about doing a little job for me?" asked Mama. "I noticed that my spice cabinet needs a good cleaning. Why don't you do that for me?"

Anna Rose thought a moment. Yes, that was the kind of job she liked to do. She liked to put things in order, just so; especially small things. She went to the kitchen and pushed one of the wooden chairs close to the place where the spice cabinet hung on the wall. Mary Elizabeth followed her.

Mama came and handed Anna Rose a soft, slightly damp cloth.

"Wipe each one and hand it down to Mary Elizabeth. Be sure the tops are closed tight before you give them to her. When you have all of them wiped and off the shelves, I'll show you how to wash the shelves. Then you can put all the spice cans back again." Mama went back to her sewing.

Anna Rose looked at the two shelves of spice cans. Most were of the same size, but the names were different.

She could not read them, but she could see that some started with A, some with B, and some with C and all kinds of letters. That gave her an idea.

"Can I put them back like the ABC song?" Anna Rose called to her mother.

"What do you mean?" Mama wanted to know.

"First an A, then a B, then a C—you know, like the song." Anna Rose sang it out for her mother.

"A, B, C, D, E, F, G," sang Mary Elizabeth.

"All right. Put them back like the ABC song," agreed Mama. "That will help me find them next time I'm looking for the spices I don't use so often."

Anna Rose began to take down the spice cans, one by one. She slid each top shut tightly. After dusting and wiping away the loose spice powder with the damp cloth, she handed them down to Mary Elizabeth. Mary Elizabeth lined them up like blocks, in rows and small towers. The bottles of vanilla and other flavorings Anna Rose did not pass down but placed them on the counter by the sink.

"I'm ready to wash the shelves," called Anna Rose. Mama came, wet a dishrag in warm water, wrung it out, and then rubbed on a little soap.

"Rub hard, like this," Mama showed her. "Be sure to wipe in all the corners."

Anna Rose washed all four corners of both shelves carefully. She wiped them dry with a dish towel. Now it was time to sort out the spice cans. First, she looked for one starting with an A. She saw two of them.

"Should I make two ABC's or should I put all the A's together and all the B's and all the C's?" Anna Rose was asking her mother when a big clap of thunder shook the house. From the back bedroom they heard Virgie wake with a cry. Mama got up from her sewing.

"Put all the A's first, then the B's, then the C's, and so on. Angeline will have to help you. I have to feed Virginia." Mama went to the bedroom to get her.

Anna Rose took the two cans with an A on them over to Angie.

"What are these called?" she asked.

"Allspice. Anise." Angie barely took time to look up from her book.

"Which one goes first?"

"Allspice. All- comes before An-." Angie answered quickly in the hope that Anna Rose would go away and not bother her more.

Anna Rose climbed back on the chair, put away the two cans, and climbed down again to search for the B's. She found two of them.

"What are these?" Anna Rose was at Angie's side again.

"Bay Leaves and Basil. And Basil comes before Bay Leaves." Angie pointed to each can with annoyance. She did not like all these interruptions.

Back to the shelf went the Basil and Bay Leaves. When Anna Rose looked for cans starting with C, she found five of them. How would she ever remember which was which?

"Angie, come and help me," begged Anna Rose. "There are five C's."

Angie pretended not to hear.

"Go and help her," Mama spoke up from the rocker where she was nursing Virgie.

With a slam, Angie put down her book on the bookcase and came to the kitchen. She plonked down the five cans, one by one, in a row on the shelf next to the Bay Leaves.

"I didn't ask you to put them in. I want to know what they are," protested Anna Rose. That was the trouble with asking for help from someone older. They would just do the thing, instead of showing you how and letting you do it yourself.

"Well, if you must know, that's Caraway, that's Cardamon, that's Cayenne Pepper, that's Cinnamon, and that's Cloves." Angie poked a finger at each can as she called out its name. Then she bent down and began to arrange the other cans Mary Elizabeth still had in small stacks on the floor.

Anna Rose looked at the Cinnamon can. "Cin-na-mon," she said slowly, accenting each syllable. She repeated it. "Cin-na-mon." All of a sudden, she knew exactly what Angie meant when she played Teacher and asked them to "sound out" a word. Over and over, Angie had said "Sound it out" when she tried to teach them to read. Before, Anna Rose had not understood what Angie meant. Now, she looked intently at the *n*'s and the *m* in Cinnamon, and she *knew*, she just *knew*, that she was "sounding it out."

"Angie, listen, I can sound it out!" cried Anna Rose. "Cin-na-mon." She pointed correctly to the Cinnamon can. Then she pointed to the next can. "Ss-l-o-v-e-s," she pronounced it letter by letter, but it did not sound right.

"No, *c* is like a *k* when it is in front of *l*," Angie explained with a smile. "Can you really sound words out by yourself now?" She could hardly believe that her teaching had had some results.

In answer, Anna Rose pointed to the next can: "D-i-ll, Dill," she read out loud. On and on she went from can to can, sounding out even the hard names like Marjoram. *J* was an easy letter to remember because of Dick

and Jane in the reader and because they had a Jane in their family.

"I think you *can* read now, all by yourself!" exclaimed Angie. She still could not believe that she had been such a successful teacher.

"Let's go try one of the harder readers," she cried, shoving the last of the spice cans and flavoring bottles into their places. Mary Elizabeth looked as though she would cry because her playthings had been taken away. Then she heard what they were talking about.

"Read!" she commanded.

Back to the bookcase went Angie, only this time she did not pick up the book she had been reading. She did not take out *More Dick and Jane Stories,* either. Instead, she picked out a much fatter reader. On the cover it said *Book Two.* She had read that aloud to her younger sisters many times, but Anna Rose did not know any of the stories by heart. There were too many words.

Quickly Angie opened the book to the first story. "Now, read," she instructed.

Anna Rose sounded out each word slowly and carefully. Sometimes she sounded out letters that were not supposed to be pronounced, and Angie corrected her.

"How can you tell when you're not supposed to sound out a letter?" Anna Rose wanted to know.

"You have to figure it out by saying the whole sentence. The other words around it give you a clue," Angie replied. She felt like the detective in the mystery book she was reading. He was always explaining things to other people, because they were not smart enough to understand on their own.

For the next half-hour, Angie listened as Anna Rose read aloud the first story in the *Book Two Reader*. Mary Elizabeth also listened carefully. She repeated all the words she could understand. She wanted to read, too, and she was sure that if she kept on repeating enough words, she would soon be able to.

The storm outside passed away. The thunder moved off into the distance, sounding fainter and fainter. The black clouds blew to the east and sunshine poured through the windows.

Mama was snoozing in the rocker, along with the baby. She woke with a start.

"Time to get dinner ready," Mama called out to Angie.

Just as Anna Rose rushed in to tell Mama the good news about learning to read, she heard a car pull up to the front gate.

"Well, for heaven's sake, what is Roman doing here at this hour of the day?" wondered Mama aloud as she looked out the door. She went out to meet him, followed by the girls.

Uncle Roman opened the car door slowly. He looked nervous and upset.

"What's the matter?" asked Mama. She could see

that something was wrong.

"There's been an accident," cried Uncle Roman, and he burst into tears. Never had the girls seen Uncle Roman cry. They stood there with eyes and mouths wide open in surprise.

Uncle Roman controlled his sobbing, wiped his eyes, and began to tell Mama something in Polish, speaking very fast. Anna Rose could only make out that it was about Grandpa Jake. Something had happened during the storm.

"Jesus, Mary, Joseph," Mama said in Polish, crossing herself. She turned to Angie. "Run and get your Pa from the barn."

Angie turned and ran as fast as she could. Millie ran right after her. Anna Rose wanted to follow her, too, to hear what she would say to Daddy. But she wanted more to stay by Mama, in case she and Uncle Roman talked some more about Grandpa.

Soon Daddy came hurrying up, followed by the two boys and Angie and Millie. Mama said something quickly to him in Polish, and then she burst into tears. This time Anna Rose could make out what she said: "Your father is dead!"

With a shocked look, Daddy turned to Uncle Roman. "What happened?" he asked. Once more Uncle Roman explained in Polish. The children stood around, looking solemn and round-eyed. When Uncle Roman had finished, Mama spoke in English.

"You go back with Roman and see if there is anything you can do, Alex. The boys can do the milking and chores." Then she turned to Uncle Roman. "Come inside and sit down while Alex changes his clothes."

When they were all in the house, Mama turned to the

children: "There was an accident today, during the storm. Your Grandpa Jake was killed by lightning." Mama could not continue, so she turned to her brother. "You explain how it happened, Roman."

With a deep sigh, Uncle Roman told them: "You know that metal brace Grandpa Jake wore on his leg, don't you? Well, he was sitting in his rocker on the front porch, waiting out the storm, when a bolt of lightning struck the brace. He was killed instantly." Uncle Roman stopped. His voice broke and he could not continue. They sat in silence.

Daddy came out of his bedroom, wearing his best suit. Soon, he and Uncle Roman drove off.

"Mama, I can read. I can sound out letters," Anna Rose said excitedly.

Mama was not listening. She looked sad and distracted. This was no time to pester her.

Angie took Anna Rose aside. "We'll show her another day how you can read by yourself," she said quietly.

"Do you think they'll let me go to school, now that I can read?"

"I don't think so," said Angie, but at Anna Rose's look of disappointment she added: "But I'll bring home all the readers for you to read. That will be almost like going to school."

"No," thought Anna Rose, "it's not the same thing at all." Still, she was glad that now she could sound out words all by herself. And now she could be the teacher for Janie and Mary Elizabeth and really, truly teach them, instead of pretending. Yes, that would be the best part about knowing how to read. She could hardly wait to start playing school again with her younger sisters.

Ghostly Games

On Thursday night, two days after Grandpa had died, all
the relatives were again gathered at the stone house. They
were there to say prayers for Grandpa and to sing. That
was called the wake.

Anna Rose had heard Mama and Daddy and some of
the aunts and uncles mention that the wake must be
quiet. It could not last far into the night, as usual.
Grandma was not supposed to have too much commotion
in the house. She had taken a turn for the worse, after
learning about the terrible accident that killed Grandpa.

As they came into the farmyard and parked their car,
an older lady got out of the car parked ahead of them.

"I hope Grandma Olszewski can lead a few songs,"

said Mama when she saw the old lady. Grandma Olszewski wasn't their real Grandma, but everyone called her that. She was Grandpa's sister. She knew hundreds of songs by heart.

Grandpa was laid out in a coffin in the front room and Mama asked them all to tiptoe in silently and say a prayer. Anna Rose said the "Our Father," to herself in Polish. She wondered if Grandpa could hear her saying it inside her mind. Only a few months ago he had listened to Janie recite it.

"Now go outside and play with your cousins," whispered Mama. "And don't make too much noise."

Solemnly they walked out the front door, being careful not to let the screen door bang. Many of their cousins were already there, but this time, instead of chattering noisily, they were sitting quietly on the front steps or on the grass. Farther down on the lawn, next to the tall poplar tree, Uncle Roman was explaining how the lightning had struck. Anna Rose decided to go nearer, so she could hear better. It was only then she noticed, in the dusky evening light, that the poplar tree had been split in half, as though someone with a gigantic hatchet had sliced it through from top to bottom.

"See where this wire clothesline is wound around the tree?" Uncle Roman explained. "As soon as the lightning hit the tree, it traveled along this wire right up to the concrete pillar on the porch, where the other end is attached." Uncle Roman pointed with his hand and started walking toward the porch. The others followed, shaking their heads but not saying much.

"When the lightning reached the end of the wire here on the pillar," Uncle Roman continued, "it flashed down to the concrete. See where it blasted out three small holes?

Then it bounced across the porch to Grandpa's metal leg brace."

Everyone looked intently at the three holes in the concrete floor of the porch. Aunt Emeline started to cry softly. Uncle Roman seemed ready to break into tears himself, so he told them quickly what the doctor and county coroner had said.

"They think he was killed instantly. Probably didn't even feel any pain."

For a moment, everyone was silent. In the hushed stillness, they could hear the faint "Cheep, cheep, cheep" of baby birds.

The sound came from an old, rusted, galvanized pail hanging between the two pillars of the porch. Grandpa had set the pail there on purpose. He had liked watching birds and was pleased they were willing to make a nest right above the spot where he sat every day. The birds came back every spring.

"Imagine that!" Uncle Roman was exclaiming. "Those little wrens were not hurt at all by the lightning, even though they were so close." He shook his head again, as though he could not understand it.

The cousins wanted to see the nest in the pail. One by one, they were allowed to stand on the concrete ledge between the pillars, to peer into the pail. In the twilight, it was hard to make out the shape and color of the birds, but Anna Rose could see at least six beady eyes. They were so tiny. Nothing had happened to the birds, but Grandpa, who was so big and tall, had been struck down in an instant. Was that what Father Gara meant when he said God watches over children and little things? When you were grown-up, he said, you had to do part of the watching yourself. If you made a mistake, was that the end of you? But how could you watch out for a bolt of lightning? It came so fast. Anna Rose sighed. It was hard to figure out what you were responsible for, and what God would take care of for you.

All the uncles and aunts and other relatives went into the house and soon their voices were joined in a steady hum of prayers.

"Let's play a game," suggested Angie.

"We're not supposed to make any noise," cautioned Imelda.

"If we play Starlight, Moonlight, we can call out the song softly," argued Angie. "We don't have to shout and holler the way we usually do."

Even the older boys thought it was a good idea. There wasn't much else they could think of, because it was getting dark. Right away, some of them offered to be Searchers. The rest of the cousins would be Ghosts.

Anna Rose was afraid they would not let her play. "Maybe they will remember that I wet my pants at the anniversary party, and think I'm still a baby," she thought. But no one mentioned the accident. Even the youngest cousins could play. They had to join a group with older ones, and stay near them.

"What will we use for home base?" asked Millie. They usually used the poplar tree. Now the top was leaning over so dangerously, they were afraid to go near it.

"How about the covered swing?" asked Laura. Aunt Sophie and Uncle Roman kept a wooden swing in the front yard. It had a roof over it and inside were two seats, facing each other. Two or three persons could sit on each seat, and both sides had to rock back and forth to get the swing going. It did not go nearly as high as the rope swings they had hanging from tree branches but it was still fun.

They all agreed that the split poplar tree was far enough away from the covered swing that it could not reach them if it toppled over. The Searchers sat in the swing, held their hands over their eyes, and counted out loud. Angie was one of them.

"Don't hide near the house because that would make too much noise if we find you there," Angie interrupted her counting to caution them.

The thirty Ghost cousins separated into five groups and each group went off to hide in a different direction. Anna Rose went with Millie and three of her cousins.

"Wait for me," Janie panted as she tried to catch up to them. Mary Elizabeth was sound asleep on one of the beds in the house, but Janie was wide awake. She wanted to join in the game.

"Don't squeak or laugh or give us away when we are hiding," warned Millie.

"I won't," Janie promised.

They walked sneakily toward the main road, circled around, and came to the granary.

"Let's hide behind these wagons and machines," whispered Millie. They crouched down low and peered through.

Faintly, across the yard, they heard the Searchers start out:

Starlight, Moonlight!
We're out to see the Ghosts tonight!
Starlight, Moonlight!
We're out to see the Ghosts tonight!

At first, the Searchers spread out toward the sheds and barns along the upper part of the farmyard, opposite the granary.

"Get ready to run for home base," whispered Millie. "Now! Go!" They leaped around the machines, crawled under the lowest wires of the fence, and headed for the swing. But there was Jim, coming straight toward them!

Anna Rose wanted to shriek and yell, but she remembered they were not supposed to make any noise. All that came out was a squeaky "Eeeeek!" Too late. Jim tagged her. Now she was a Searcher, too.

They played quite a few rounds before all the Ghosts were caught. It was time for Anna Rose to be a Ghost again. She went off with Angie and her group this time. They walked to the main road, also, but came up around behind the garden. Now the front lawn was between them and the farmyard.

"We'll hide behind these raspberry bushes," whispered Angie.

"Aren't we too close to the house?" asked Anna Rose.

"This isn't near the house, it's near the garden," Angie reassured them.

From the open windows of the front room floated the hushed sound of voices, singing in a subdued way, as if they were holding back part of the song. Grandma Olszewski led each verse in her clear, sweet voice. The others would follow as soon as she gave them the first few words. On some verses, only the men sang, deep and low and mournful. When the women sang alone, it was soft and high and sad, too, but in a different way.

Suddenly, across the front yard came the voices of the Searchers, chanting as they set out:

Starlight, Moonlight!
We're out to see the Ghosts tonight!

Again and again they repeated it. The lively rhythm contrasted with the solemn, measured beat of the singers inside. The pungent scent of the ripening raspberries joined with the waves of music coming from both sides. Overhead the sparkling stars of the warm August night made just enough light to cast shadows, but not enough to see things clearly. It was so mysterious and beautiful that Anna Rose did not want to play the game any more. She wanted to sit and listen and feel.

When one of the Searchers came toward their hiding place, she only pretended to run away. As soon as she was tagged, Anna Rose said: "I'm tired. I'm going into the house."

But she was not really tired. She walked to the front porch and sat in Grandpa's rocker. Rocking slowly, she let the music and the chant of the game fill her up, until at last, she did get tired, and fell asleep.

Oatmeal Cookie Surprise

No sooner had the funeral ended for Grandpa than they had to get ready for another. Grandma died in her sleep, the day after Grandpa was buried.

"It's a blessing she went so quick. Now she won't have to suffer any more," Mama said.

The funerals were sad, but they were happy, too. The children played with their cousins. The uncles and aunts and great-uncles and great-aunts sat around most of the day, talking of the good old days. It was like an extra holiday. They only did the necessary work.

Then, for the rest of August, they were busy getting in the second crop of hay and threshing the oats. Threshing was exciting because the whole crew had to work fast and hard. Dorothy and Aunt Stella came over to help Mama and the girls make mountains of food and huge pots of coffee and pitcher after pitcher of lemonade.

It was late in the evening when they finished the threshing. The men moved the machine to the farm where the oats fields were ready to thresh next. Daddy came in with a satisfied look on his face.

"That was a good clean threshing we had. We got almost fifty bushels to the acre this year. You girls did a fine job of cleaning out those thistles."

Millie grinned proudly. Angie smiled and glanced at Anna Rose.

"What time are you leaving for Glenzinski's tomorrow morning?" Mama wanted to confirm her plans. "Eligia wants me to come and help her. I think I'll take Angeline along, so she can look after the children. Francis can come along, too, to help with the loading. Lawrence, you will have to manage here by yourself."

In the morning, very early, Mama and Daddy and Angie and Francis walked to the car. Mama had Virgie in her arms.

"Be sure to watch Mary Elizabeth and Jane," Mama called to Millie. "Anna Rose, you help her. Lawrence, keep an eye on things. We may be back quite late."

When they had left, Lawrence went to the summer kitchen, filled the stove with chunks of wood, and closed the damper.

"That should keep it until this afternoon. Now, don't touch the stove or put in any more wood," he told Millie. "I'll come and check it again after I clean out the barn."

All morning the girls played in the house or the backyard. They did not have to pick nettles because the geese were now old enough to tear off the leaves by themselves. They did not have to carry wood, because the stove in the summer kitchen used only a small stack of wood each day. They did not have to weed in the garden any more, because everything was almost full grown and ready for harvest. The middle of August was full of fun time.

At noon, Lawrence came in and helped Millie slice bread and tomatoes and cucumbers. There was food left over from the big threshing meals of the day before so they did not have to cook anything. Lawrence and Millie put the bowls and platters in the center of the table and everyone reached for the food. It was like a picnic.

"I still have the bull pen to clean up, but then I'll come and make a surprise," announced Lawrence after they had finished eating.

"What? What?" clamored the four girls, all at the same time.

"Wait and see, wait and see," Lawrence teased them.

Mary Elizabeth did not want to take her nap, so Millie led the three girls to the couch in the front room. She fixed up some pillows for Janie and Mary Elizabeth to lean against, and began to read a long story. By the end of it, both girls were fast asleep.

Millie and Anna Rose were deciding what to play next when Lawrence returned. First, he went to the summer kitchen, opened the damper and put more sticks of wood in the stove. Then he came back to the kitchen and took out the large, white enamel bowl in which Mama mixed her bread dough.

"Are you going to make bread?" Anna Rose asked in surprise.

"Nope. But I *am* going to make a b-i-g batch of oatmeal cookies." The way Lawrence stretched out the words showed the girls he was talking about a *lot* of cookies.

81

"Did Mama say you should?" asked Millie.

"She didn't say I couldn't!" Lawrence laughed smugly. "They are having good things to eat with the threshing crew. We can have our own treat."

Anna Rose and Millie looked up at their brother doubtfully. They had just finished a meal of all sorts of delicious things. They were not sure what Mama would think of Lawrence's surprise. He paid no attention to their questioning looks, but started mixing a batter for the oatmeal cookies. Butter, sugar, eggs, flour, oatmeal, soda, and salt. One after the other he beat them until they made a thick, oozy mass. Last of all, he added a heaping cupful of chopped hickory nuts from the jar where Mama kept them, high up in the cupboard.

Taking a teaspoon, he spooned out twenty-four small mounds on a baking sheet, and then slid it into the oven.

"I may not have them just right. We'll bake one pan and taste them before we put in any more." Lawrence's eyes sparkled in anticipation. Anna Rose and Millie could hardly wait for the fifteen minutes to be over.

At last, the pan was ready to come out of the oven. The cookies looked crispy and brown at the edges. Lawrence loosened them from the sheet with a pancake turner. He picked up one of the cookies, juggled it back and forth in his hands until it was cool, and then bit into it. From the smile on his face, Anna Rose and Millie could see that it tasted good.

"Get a pitcher of milk from the cellar," Lawrence told Millie. He took out three mugs and filled them with the cool milk as soon as Millie brought it. They each took two cookies and ate them, alternating the warm bites with cool swallows of milk. They each took two more, and then two more. Anna Rose and Millie were full. They could not eat another bite. But Lawrence kept on munching cookies until he had finished the whole pan. Just as he began to prepare the cookie sheet to bake another batch, they heard the sound of the dogs barking and a car pulling up at the gate. Lawrence opened the door to look out.

"Holy smoke! What are they doing back already?" He looked at the unbaked cookie dough. "I'll bet something went wrong on the machine and they have to wait to get it fixed. Listen," Lawrence continued, "let this be our secret. We can bake the rest when they go off tomorrow. Millie, wash that pan, quick, before they come inside. I'll go hide the cookie dough. Mind, not a word! Can you keep a secret?" he asked Anna Rose.

She nodded her head. While Lawrence snuck out the side door, Millie rinsed the baking sheet in the sink and dried it with the dishcloth. She had barely put it away in a pantry cupboard when Mama and Angie came in.

"A part broke on the machine. It will take them the rest of today to get it welded and fixed," Mama explained.

The next day, after breakfast, Mama did not get ready to go.

"Aren't you going to Glenzinski's today?" asked Millie.

"We got all the baking and cooking done yesterday. Eligia said she could manage by herself today. Lawrence, you go with Pa and Francis. We'll manage the chores by ourselves for once."

Lawrence opened his mouth as if to say something, but no words came out. Then he winked at Anna Rose. That meant he would think of another way to carry out their secret.

Saturday came, and still they had not been alone long enough to finish the cookies.

"Has anyone seen my enamel bread bowl?" asked Mama. There was silence in the kitchen. Lawrence was not there.

"For heaven's sake, it can't have disappeared just like that. Millie, did you use it the day we were gone?"

Millie hesitated, then shook her head. "No, I didn't use it." Well, that was the truth, but only part of it. It was wrong to tell a lie. This was not exactly a lie, though it was not the whole truth, either.

Grumbling to herself, Mama took out another pan, one she did not like as well. She mixed the bread in it, and made the snail dough in the large crockery bowl, as usual.

Still another day went by. Anna Rose wondered where the oatmeal cookie dough was hidden and what would happen to it. Lawrence did not seem to be worried. He gave her a wink every time no one was looking.

On Monday morning, Anna Rose was playing with Millie and Janie on the swing. It hung from a tall tree, not far from the corncrib. They saw Daddy come to the corncrib with a sack in his hands.

"Jingers, crackers! What did I step in here?" they heard Daddy call out. In a moment, he appeared at the corncrib door, and the girls began to giggle. On one foot, Daddy had his shoe stuck in Mama's white enamel bowl. It was held tight in the gooey, sticky mess that had once been the dough for oatmeal cookies. At first, Daddy looked angry. Then, he started to laugh.

Clump! Clump! Clump! He hobbled up to the side kitchen door.

"Look how I found your bread bowl, Anna!" he called to Mama.

Mama was speechless. She could not even ask where Daddy had found it. He looked so funny, she started to

chuckle, and then to laugh. The tears streamed down her cheeks and she lifted her apron to wipe them away. Daddy unstuck his shoe and began to clean it off with an old rag. Mama scraped the oozing mess from the bowl into the slop pail, laughing all the while.

"I think you had better call Lawrence and tell him to come here," she said at last to Anna Rose.

Lawrence came to the kitchen door. He took one look at the bowl in Mama's hands and his face flushed a bright red.

"How did you know it was me?" asked Lawrence.

"Who else could it have been?" Mama replied. "You're the one who is always up to mischief. If you like making oatmeal cookies so much, I think I will let you do the baking this Saturday, from morning to night." Mama's voice was scolding, but she was half smiling. She gave him a big spank with the bottom of the bowl.

Santa Claus
and Angel Wings

In September, school started again for her older sisters and brothers, but Anna Rose was not allowed to go. Mama said she was not ready.

"Mama, I am *too* ready for school," insisted Anna Rose. "I can read the second grade book all the way through."

Mama thought for a while. "All right. I'll let you go to school with Angeline next week and you can read for Sister Pelagia, the principal. Maybe she will let you start before you are six."

Anna Rose was delighted. At last she was getting a chance to go to school.

"I know what I'll do. I'll practice my reading so I can

86

do it just right, without stopping. Will you help me, Angie?"

All day Saturday and Sunday, whenever they had a free moment, Anna Rose practiced reading aloud to Angie.

The following Monday, she went to school with Angie, carrying a letter from Mama to the principal. Shortly after they arrived, Sister Pelagia read the letter and then asked Anna Rose to read from two different books. She nodded and smiled as Anna Rose sounded out the words, hardly stumbling at all.

"You read very nicely," said Sister Pelagia. "Now take a seat next to your sister and stay there quietly."

"She looks pleased," thought Anna Rose. "I wonder if that means I can come every day after this?" For the rest of that day, she sat next to Angie, practicing her letters and reading silently from different books. Sometimes she stopped to listen to the seventh or eighth graders recite. At the end of the school day, Sister Pelagia asked Angie to wait for a few minutes.

"I want to send a note to your mother."

Anna Rose watched as she wrote carefully on a sheet of white paper, folded it, and sealed it in an envelope. As she handed the envelope to Angie, Sister Pelagia smiled at Anna Rose.

"She's going to let me come!" Anna Rose felt sure that was what the smile meant.

But when Mama opened the note and read it, she shook her head.

"Sister Pelagia says you must wait until next year. She says if she makes an exception for you, all the parents will ask her to let their children come to school before they are six. We must abide by the rules, she says."

Bitterly disappointed, Anna Rose turned aside to hide

her tears. That was the last time she would trust Sister Pelagia's smile.

"Why don't you play School with Jane and Mary Elizabeth?" suggested Mama.

"I already played School with them. They don't sit still," complained Anna Rose.

Mama thought for a moment. "I think you need a special place that *looks* like school. I'll fix you a nice corner in the attic for your classroom."

The front part of the attic was a bedroom where Lawrence and Francis slept. In the back part was a storage place for trunks and boxes and all sorts of interesting things. Mama did not usually let them play there. Now she emptied one corner, pushing all the boxes to the other side. She placed a large square trunk right below the window, and put a chair behind it.

"My grandma brought this trunk from Poland, so don't pound on it or mark it up," cautioned Mama. "You can use it as a desk as long as you take care of it." Then Mama stood two wooden egg crates up on their ends.

"These will be desks for Jane and Mary Elizabeth. See, there is a shelf inside each one where they can keep

their papers and a pencil and crayons. They can sit on that nice little bench we have. I'll let you bring it up from the summer kitchen."

Every day after that, the three girls played School, for at least a short while. When they got tired of playing School, they played Store or Doctor or House. Mama said she was glad because that kept them out of mischief.

Before they realized it, Christmas was approaching. It was time to butcher the geese. Mama knew how to do it, with Angie and Lawrence and Francis to help her. Anna Rose and Millie had to help pluck the feathers. They were not one bit sorry to get rid of those pesky geese.

"Why don't we butcher that mean gander?" asked Anna Rose.

"We have to save a few geese and the gander so there will be eggs to hatch out again next spring," Mama explained. She stuffed the feathers loosely in some flour sacks and Millie carried them up to the attic where they would be left to dry for a few months.

Mama saved one plump goose for the family to eat on Christmas Day. The rest she sold to her regular customers in town and came back with more than a hundred dollars.

"Now I have my Christmas money. I can go on a shopping spree," Mama gloated with satisfaction.

"Don't forget the rope tinsel for my angel costume," Millie reminded her. Millie was going to be an angel in the Christmas pageant at school and again at Midnight Mass on Christmas Eve.

When Daddy and Mama came home from shopping one week before Christmas, they brought strands of tinsel and rope tinsel; a box of shiny, colored balls; small wax candles; colored tissue paper and thin gold string. Best of all, Daddy brought in a bushel basket of bright, golden-orange tangerines. They could each eat one every day, even though it was Advent and they were not allowed to have candy or sweets. There were also other packages that Mama did not let the children open. These she hid in her bedroom.

Mama sewed the silvery rope tinsel around the neck and sleeves of the long white dress Millie was going to wear. She measured and cut a long piece to tie around Millie's waist. On the last day of school before Christmas vacation started, Millie took the dress with her, in a box. Mama and Daddy did not go to school to see the pageant, because they were too busy to make a special trip all the way to Pine Creek. They would see Millie on Christmas Eve.

"I wish it would snow so we could take the sleigh," Anna Rose prayed as she looked out the window the night before Christmas Eve. But it did not snow the next day. It was clear and cold and crisp. Not a snowflake was in sight.

That night, they sat down to supper earlier than usual. Lawrence was not there.

"Aren't we going to wait for Lawrence?" asked Anna Rose.

"He is going to finish the milking and separating by himself. We have to get washed and dressed." Daddy had a twinkle in his eyes as he spoke.

"That's not fair," thought Anna Rose. "Lawrence has to do the work all alone."

They were finishing their prayer after supper when a jingling of bells sounded outside the kitchen door.

"Who can that be?" Mama wondered aloud.

"I think it must be Santa Claus! He came early because he knew we were going to church early, to see the pageant," Daddy exclaimed. Anna Rose looked back and forth at Mama and Daddy, and at Angie, Millie, and

Francis. They were smiling at each other and their sparkly eyes seemed to be sharing a secret. Mama opened the door and in walked Santa Claus, tall and bearded. He did not seem to be as fat as some of the Santas pictured in the newspaper.

Janie was not scared of him. She walked up and shook his hand. Mary Elizabeth and Anna Rose stayed close to Mama. Virgie was learning to walk and when Santa held out his arms, she waddled over. Then she walked unsteadily back to Daddy.

As Santa handed presents to every person around the table, he talked in a gruff voice. He asked Angie if she had been a good girl all year. Then he asked the others the same question. Anna Rose wondered about Lawrence. So far, there was no present for him. Had he been too mischievous last year? That was not fair. He liked to have fun, that was all.

"You didn't forget a present for Lawrence, did you? cried Anna Rose.

"I certainly did not forget him," Santa laughed as he shook his head. He was not speaking in such a gruff voice now. "Such a good boy, finishing the milking all by himself." Santa put a large box on the table. "Be sure to give it to him as soon as he comes in," he told Anna Rose. Then Santa left, jingling his bells.

"I have heard that voice before," thought Anna Rose. She wondered if it was the same Santa as last year.

They put the presents under the tree and went to do dishes. Before long, Lawrence came in, carrying the empty milk pails to be washed out.

"Already?" he exclaimed in surprise when they told him Santa had been there.

"He left a big package for you. He said you were a good boy," Anna Rose assured him.

Mama put the new candles in the metal holders and clipped them on to the tree branches. She put them at the tip of each branch, where they would not touch the needles or wood. Carefully, Mama lit each candle. Daddy kept a pail of sand and a bucket of water off to the side to throw on the tree if it caught fire. But Mama watched very carefully and as soon as any candle burned down close to the holder, she snuffed it out.

Watching the flickering candles, they sang one Christmas song after another. Some they sang in English and others in Polish. When the last candle had been snuffed out, Mama lit the lamps.

"Now you may open the presents." Mama gave the signal by lifting Virgie to her lap and putting a present in front of her. When Virgie tore off the wrapping, they could see a soft, plushy doll. It looked partly like a baby and partly like a rabbit. It was called a Bye Baby Bunting Doll.

Mary Elizabeth, Janie, and Anna Rose each got a doll, too. They were different sizes and had different colored hair. Those were the first brand-new dolls they had ever had. All the other dolls they played with were left over from the time when Angie and Millie were little.

The girls were so engrossed in their new dolls, they paid no attention to the other gifts, and before they knew what was happening, Mama was bundling them up in their warm clothes. Soon they were in the car, riding off to the pageant and to Midnight Mass. Millie went down to the church basement while the rest climbed the steps to the church.

They did not have to wait long for the pageant to start. Millie looked beautiful as she came walking down the aisle. Wound around her blond hair was a tinsel halo. As soon as she came near the pew in which they were sitting, Anna Rose could see the wings attached to Millie's back and shoulders.

"They have real feathers!" whispered Anna Rose to Angie. Millie kept her eyes cast down and her hands folded. She did not smile as she passed their pew. Some of the other girls giggled when they walked by their families, but Millie went up the aisle looking angelic all the way.

"Some day I'm going to be an angel," Anna Rose told Angie in a long, sighing whisper.

"You'll get your turn in third grade. Now be quiet, they're going to start speaking their parts."

All through the pageant and the Mass, Anna Rose did not take her eyes off the angel wings. Her younger sisters had fallen asleep but she was wide awake. She wanted to see every move the angels made. If she remembered them next year, maybe they would let her be an angel in the first grade. Then she would not have to wait until third grade.

Anna Rose went home with the family in a daze. In her sleep she dreamed she was an angel with real wings, flying with her new doll over the heads of all the people in church, high up into the highest corners. When she woke up, she could hardly remember where she was.

"No doubt about it," Anna Rose thought. "That means I will be an angel in the pageant next year." It was the best ending to Christmas Eve she ever had.

The Feather Monsters

January was cold and full of snowstorms. Many mornings, Mama asked Anna Rose to watch her sisters while she went down to the cellar alone to do the separating. Sometimes, the snow blew so fast and thick that the older children did not go to school. Daddy was afraid they would not be able to get through to the main road. Those days were fun. They played with their new dolls and Angie read aloud all the stories from her new reading book. Daddy brought out the harmonica and they sang and danced. Not much work could be done. They milked the cows, fed the animals and brought in wood, but that was about all.

One evening in February, Mama went to the attic and

brought down a sack of goose feathers. She plunged her hand deep inside and brought out a few. Holding one by the tip, she stripped the flat white sides from the center shaft, first one, then the other.

"They are dry enough for stripping," said Mama. "We will strip some every evening. It is a good job for Lent."

She cleared the kitchen table and wiped it dry. In the center, she made a small pile of fluffy white feathers. Everyone sat down in a chair and began stripping. Strip! Strip! Throw away the shaft with the quill on the end. Strip! Strip! Throw away. Over and over again. There were thousands and thousands of feathers to strip.

Daddy started singing and they joined in. He liked to sing religious songs during Lent. They were not as lively as the other Polish songs. Daddy and the boys and Millie sang low. Mama and the other girls sang high. The harmony was calm and soothing. The stripped feather piles in front of each place began to grow. Soon they had finished the pile in the middle. Mama collected the stripped feathers in a clean pillowcase. The bare quills she wrapped in some old newspapers.

"Aren't you going to throw those in the fire?" asked Anna Rose as she saw her mother put the package off to the side of the wood bin.

"Oh, no! Feathers give off an awful stink when they burn," Mama explained. "We'll throw them on the junk pile in the big ditch as soon as the weather is better."

Every night they stripped feathers and sang. Mama filled four clean pillowcases with the soft feathers.

"I do believe I'll soon have enough to make another feather quilt," said Mama. "We don't need any more pillows right now, but an extra feather quilt would come in handy."

By the week before Easter, there was less than half a sack of feathers left to strip. That night, after supper, Mama and Daddy got dressed in their Sunday clothes.

"We are going to say prayers at the wake for Vince Bambenek. Try to finish the feather stripping tonight. We have a lot of cleaning and decorating to do next week." Mama got them settled at their places by the table before she left the house.

For a while they stripped quietly. No one felt like starting a song. They were tired of stripping feathers.

"I'm thirsty," Lawrence said as he got up. He was about to turn on the water when he saw the milk pitcher at the side of the sink. There was milk left inside, from supper. Lawrence drank down a tall glassful.

"You have a milk mustache," laughed Anna Rose, pointing to his mouth.

Lawrence looked in the mirror of the medicine chest and made a face. He went to the table, picked up two feathers, and pasted them on his upper lip. One of the tips stuck out to the left. The other tip stuck out to the right. The leftover milk made the feathers stay on his face, giving him a silly feather mustache.

"I want a mustache, too," giggled Anna Rose. She went to the pitcher, took a big swallow of milk, and let the milk drip out around her lips. She picked up two feathers and put them over her upper lip, slanting downward. It looked just like Grandpa's mustache used to look.

Now the others wanted to try on feather mustaches. They gulped swallows of milk, letting it flow over the edge of the glass and onto their upper lips. Each pasted on a feather mustache, one more comical than the other. They looked at each other and howled and hooted.

The milk dried and the feathers fell off.

"I have an idea," said Lawrence. He went into the

pantry and brought out a bowl with syrup. After poking his finger into the syrup, he spread dabs of it over his chin and cheeks. Quickly he fastened feathers over the syrupy spots.

"Look at my beard. I'm a wise old one," he bragged.

Of course, the rest had to try that, too. They smeared syrup over their faces and plastered feathers on, as many as would catch hold. Francis put them on his forehead and ears, too. He got so much syrup on his hands, the feathers stuck as much to his fingers as to his face.

"Grrrrr! I'm a feather monster," he growled and came at Anna Rose on all fours. She shrieked and ran to the other side of the table.

"Ssshh! Not so loud. You'll wake up the little ones," warned Angie.

Soon they were all feather monsters, sticking the white, downy pieces to any part of their skin that was bare. They rolled on the floor, pretending to fight each other. They chased each other around and around the

table, growling and spitting like wildcats. The feathers began to fall off. Francis reached out to replace some of his.

"Oh, my gosh! Ma is going to wonder what happened to all the feathers." They looked and saw that the pile in the center of the table was half the size it was when they had started and there were almost no stripped feathers in front of each place. They began to tear off the sticky feathers. They could not strip them. All the other feathers would stick to them, instead of staying white and dry and fluffy.

"What will we do with them?" Angie wondered.

"Burn them!" answered Lawrence.

"Mama says feathers stink when they burn," warned Anna Rose.

"I know they do, but we can't wrap them in newspaper to throw away later. Ma would see them. We'll burn them and leave the door open to get rid of the smell," Lawrence reassured them.

It took a long time to pull the sticky feathers away from their faces and fingers. Finally they managed to pile them in one gummy lump on some newspaper. They washed their hands and faces and scrubbed away all the syrup from the floor. Lawrence folded up the newspaper and stuffed the lumpy package into the kitchen stove.

"Are you sure that will burn?" asked Angie.

"Sure, sure." Lawrence was very confident. "Let's get to work and finish stripping the rest."

Before long, a terrible, acrid smell filled the kitchen.

"Pee-yew!" Francis wrinkled his nose disgustedly. "I thought you said it wouldn't smell."

"No, I said we could open the door to get rid of the smell." Lawrence went to the kitchen door and opened it wide. A cold blast of air blew in. It took away some of the smell, but it also sent the feathers flying into the air in all directions, like puffs of smoke.

"Shut the door!" cried Angie.

Lawrence shut the door and they scrambled about, collecting the feathers that were floating in every corner. When most of them were on the table again, they began to strip in earnest.

Soon the smell got strong again. They could hardly stand it.

"Maybe if I open the door part-way it won't blow the feathers away." Lawrence jumped up and opened the door a few inches. The draft sucked around the edges of the walls, pulling the feathers from the table top. A few landed on top of the stove. Immediately they began to turn brown and smell even worse than the feathers burning inside.

"Shut it all the way!" they cried. They would have to strip all the feathers first and put them safely away in the pillow case. Then they could open the door and air out the kitchen.

Swiftly they stripped, their nimble fingers going as fast as they could. It was late when they finally came to the bottom of the pile. Millie held the pillowcase at the edge of the table and Angie neatly slid the piles of stripped feathers inside. They wrapped the discarded quills in newspaper and put the bundle next to the woodbin.

"Now, open the door and all the windows," ordered Lawrence. He shook down the ashes in the stove, piled in more wood, and got the fire burning hot and fast. The others opened every window and door and then waved dish towels through the air, forcing the smell outside. It got chilly in the kitchen and front room, but Lawrence would not let them close any windows until he was satisfied that most of the smell was gone.

The dogs barked and car headlights swerved up and around to the main gate. Lawrence closed the door with a bang, and the others each rushed to close a window. A few minutes later, Mama and Daddy walked in.

"Are you all still up? It didn't take you so long to do the feathers, did it?" No one answered Mama. "Brrrr! It's so chilly in here. Did you forget the fire?" asked Mama.

"I did let it run down kind of low," admitted Lawrence. "But now it's burning just fine."

Sniff, sniff! Mama's nose caught the lingering smell of burned feathers. "Did you put the quills in the fire?" she asked suspiciously.

"No, Ma. Here they are. When I opened the door once, some feathers blew away and landed on the stove," explained Lawrence, with an innocent look on his face. "They burned up before we could get them brushed off. You must be smelling that."

Mama looked at all their faces.

"Well, I don't know what it was, but you all look as though you have been up to some mischief." Mama walked into the pantry. "Did you sneak something to eat?" she asked accusingly. They were not supposed to eat between meals during Lent.

"No, Mama, honest, we didn't eat a thing!" Anna Rose spoke the truth. She was glad she could be so convincing without telling a lie.

"Well, if you weren't in the pantry getting something to eat, how did this feather get into the syrup bowl?" Mama asked with a laugh.

"Oh, you know how feathers can fly. It must have blown there in the draft from the open door," Lawrence explained. With a laugh he started up the stairs. The others followed behind, giggling and tittering.

Dyngus

On Thursday of Holy Week, the week before Easter, they washed clothes and curtains and sheets and towels and rugs. On Good Friday, before going to church, they cleaned the house from top to bottom and put the clean rugs on the floor, the curtains on the windows, and the sheets on the beds. On Saturday, Mama baked all day. By late afternoon, the pantry shelves were filled with fresh loaves of bread, snails, and square, plump doughnuts. Mama called the doughnuts *ponchki*. Anna Rose could never decide which tasted better: the cinnamon and raisin flavored snails with the vanilla frosting, or the *ponchki* with their crispy outer crust covered with sugar.

On Saturday evening, Mama brought out as many

old cups and jars as she could find. She poured in hot water until each cup or jar was half full; then she added drops of food coloring. There were only four colors in the bottles: red, yellow, blue, and green. But Mama knew how to mix red and yellow to make orange. With red and blue drops she made violet. To make brown, she put in drops of red and yellow and blue. Finally, she placed a large bowl of hard-boiled eggs in the center of the table.

Each of the children could dye four or five eggs, choosing any color combinations they wished. Angie made swirls and patterns by dipping only part of an egg in at one time, first in one color and then in another. Anna Rose let her eggs stay in the dye for only a short time. When she took them out and dried them on an old rag, they looked like pastel candies of pale pink, blue, yellow, green, and lilac. Millie did the opposite. She let her eggs stay in a long time and when they were ready, each was a deep, vibrant color.

After they had completed dying the eggs, they placed them in their Easter baskets and left them in the center of the table. During the night the Easter Bunny would put so many candy eggs in each basket, the real eggs would be almost covered up.

Lawrence watched as the others dyed their eggs and prepared their baskets. He did not color a single egg.

"Aren't you going to color any Easter eggs?" Anna Rose asked him.

"I don't need to. I know a better way to get them," Lawrence answered.

"The Easter Bunny won't bring you any candy," teased Mama.

"Oh, I don't care. I'll manage to get some, you'll see." Lawrence smiled and seemed unconcerned.

The next morning, when they came down to breakfast, the Easter baskets were full to the top with candy eggs. There were chocolate eggs and marshmallow eggs and jelly bean eggs. Propped in the middle of each basket was a small chocolate rabbit. Only Lawrence had no basket. Off to the side was a lone chocolate rabbit. That was all the candy he got. Anna Rose and Millie felt sorry for him.

"Here, you can have one of my marshmallow eggs and one of my chocolate eggs," offered Anna Rose. Millie gave him a marshmallow egg and a handful of jelly beans.

"That's nice of you, but you really don't have to worry about me," insisted Lawrence. "I still intend to get my share of candy." But he did not refuse the offerings of his sisters. He ate them up as soon as they had returned from church.

The girls and Francis nibbled at their candies on and off all day. They each cracked a real egg and ate it with salt and pepper. By evening, their baskets were still more than half full. The candy and eggs would last them all week.

Early on Monday morning, Anna Rose heard Angie and Millie get up. There were morning chores to do, even though they did not have to go to school.

"Eeeek! Help!" Shrieks and hollers came from the other side of the house, near the kitchen door. Anna Rose jumped out of bed and went to the window. She could not see a thing but she could hear Angie and Millie yelling and yelping. She could also hear Lawrence calling out something, but it was impossible to make out the words.

Quickly Anna Rose got dressed and ran down the stairs. Mama was seated at the kitchen table, smiling and sipping her coffee.

"What is going on?" asked Anna Rose.

In answer, the door burst open and Angie and Millie

ran in. They were dripping wet. Anna Rose looked out the window at the bright sunshine.

"How did you get so wet if it is not raining?" she asked.

Both Angie and Millie were giggling so hard they could not answer. At last Angie spoke.

"It is showering outside."

Once more Anna Rose looked out the window. All she could see was blue sky and bright sunshine.

"There is not a drop of a shower in sight," she insisted.

"If you don't believe us, go outside and see," Millie said, wiping her hair with a towel.

Anna Rose marched to the kitchen door, opened it, and stepped outside onto the short sidewalk that led to the woodpile and gate. She had not gone more than three steps when a shower of water swooshed over her head. It dripped onto her face and down her body. Lawrence's voice called out from behind the woodpile:

Dyngus, Dyngus, po dwa jaja!
Nie chc chleba tylko jaja!

Dingus, Dingus, for two eggs!
Don't give me bread, only eggs!

Lawrence stepped out with the hose in one hand and a switch of willow branches in the other. He swatted her with the branches and continued to sprinkle her as she tried to run away. She squealed and yelled: "Turn it off!"

"Promise to give me two eggs."

"I promise!" screamed Anna Rose. The water was cold and tingly. As soon as Lawrence turned it off, Anna Rose went back into the kitchen to dry off.

"So *that* is how Lawrence is getting his Easter candy," she said.

"You did not remember about *Dyngus* Monday," laughed Mama, "because the last time Lawrence did that, you were only three years old."

"What is *Dyngus?*" asked Anna Rose.

"It's just a custom we have from the old country," explained Mama. "On Easter Monday the boys give the girls a switching and a sprinkling of water and in exchange they want eggs or candies."

When Mary Elizabeth and Janie got up, Lawrence did the same thing to them. He only gave them a light spanking and a quick sprinkling, so as not to scare them, but he insisted they each give him two candy eggs from their baskets. They did not like it, but Mama agreed those were the rules. By the end of the day he had eaten eight candy eggs and four colored eggs.

"That's not fair," cried Angie. "Now he got more than any of us."

"Aren't you forgetting about tomorrow?" Mama reminded her that Easter Tuesday was the day for girls to play *Dyngus* on the boys.

"But how can we get back any eggs? He ate them already," complained Millie.

"Never mind that," Angie dismissed the complaint with a wave of her hand. "We still have pretty many jelly beans and eggs. The important thing is to give him a good soaking and a switching."

"I think you will have a hard time catching him," chuckled Mama. "He will be on the lookout for you all day."

That evening Anna Rose huddled in bed next to Angie and Millie. In whispers, they made their plans for the next day.

"Are you sure you can keep after Lawrence while we make our preparations?" Angie asked Anna Rose.

"I know just what to do," she assured her sisters.

On Tuesday morning, Lawrence got up very early. He was out of the house before any of his sisters were awake. In the barn he knew he was safe because Pa would not let them fool around while they were near the cows.

"Bring me a hunk of bread and jam," he said to Francis. "I don't trust those girls to let me in for breakfast without getting a sprinkle." Francis brought him two thick slices of bread with jam between them.

All morning, Lawrence worked in the barn, cleaning out the gutters and stanchions. He shoveled the manure out the back door, into the manure spreader. Once or twice, he came to the front door and peeked out. He could see Anna Rose standing there, holding a sprinkling can.

Close to noon, Lawrence began to get really hungry.

"Aw, c'mon," he called. "Let me go by!"

"I'm not leaving here until you leave the barn," Anna Rose informed him.

"We'll see about that," Lawrence laughed in reply. He went to the back barn door, stepped out, and slowly walked to the lower corner. Peering around it, he could see that the front door to the house was unguarded.

"I can run faster than any of them," he said to himself. "I'll go in that door." He raced toward it, opened it quickly, and entered the house.

"Ha! Ha! You didn't get me," crowed Lawrence gleefully, when he saw Angie and Millie setting the table. They just smiled back at him.

Anna Rose came in the door. She was smiling smugly.

"Aren't you mad that I snuck by you?" asked Lawrence.

Anna Rose did not answer. She just kept on smiling as if she had a secret. Angie and Millie were also silent.

Lawrence was puzzled. His sisters seemed so confident. He had better watch more carefully than ever.

They laughed and joked at the dinner table. When they were finished, Angie moved over toward the kitchen door.

"Oh, no you don't," cried Lawrence as he ran for the door ahead of her. "I'm going out first." Lawrence turned the knob and pulled the door open. In the same moment, Angie stooped and pulled a string lying loose at the left edge of the door sill.

Splash! Lawrence stepped out into a torrent of water.

The pail that Angie and Millie had rigged up over the kitchen door emptied out completely, right over his head. Millie ran to get the willow switches they had prepared and began to switch Lawrence on his legs and backside.

"Tee, hee! We fooled you!" Anna Rose cackled and danced with merriment. "We *wanted* you to come in the front door. Angie said you would, if I could stand at the front barn door all morning with a sprinkler, and I did. We didn't want you to see the pail."

Lawrence came back into the kitchen, shaking his head to get the water out of his eyes. As he reached for the roller towel, he could hear the kitchen exploding with hilarity.

"Serves you right," Daddy said cheerfully. "Don't try to get the better of these girls. They are too smart. And besides, you're outnumbered."

Dress Up

"It's raining again. We won't be able to work in the garden." Mama sounded disappointed. The last two weeks in April seemed like one long rainstorm. The older children grumbled about having to ride in the open buggy in the rain. Lawrence was not there to cheer them up with his jokes and tricks. He was living in Winona for six weeks, while taking a special course in mechanics.

Anna Rose did not like so much rain, either. It meant she had to watch her younger sisters and play with them inside the house. Virgie was hard to keep track of, now that she was walking. She was curious about everything and had to be watched every minute.

Mama was making bread that rainy day. Clickety-snickety, clickety-snickety went the flour sifter as she sprinkled more flour over the lump of dough. She set down the flour sifter at the edge of the table and turned to the stove. After fitting a curved handle into one of the round lids, Mama lifted it to the side.

"Guess I'd better put more wood on the fire if I want the oven hot enough to bake bread," she said.

Anna Rose was only half listening. She and Janie and Mary Elizabeth were absorbed in their dolls. They were getting them dressed in the fresh, clean dresses Angie had ironed for them yesterday.

While Mama's back was turned, Virgie reached for the sifter. The "clickety-snickety" noise had made her curious. She stretched her hand as far as she could. Her fingertips could just reach the sifter handle. As she pulled it toward her, it tipped over.

Poof! A cloud of flour showered down on Virgie and spread over the kitchen floor. The sifter dropped to the floor with a bang. Virgie began to cry.

"Oh, no! Weren't you watching her?" scolded Mama.

Anna Rose looked up guiltily from her doll. She had forgotten to keep her eyes on what Virgie was doing.

"Well, if you don't look like a snow girl," laughed Mama, brushing the flour from Virgie's face with a towel. Virgie stopped crying and started giggling. She liked being a snow girl now that the flour was no longer in her eyes.

Mama took off Virgie's dress and gave it a good shake outside the kitchen door, without stepping into the rain. Then she cleaned up the mess from the kitchen floor. Anna Rose helped her by holding the dustpan.

"Go up in the attic to play," pleaded Mama.

"Virgie won't sit still when we play School," complained Anna Rose. She was tired of playing School, anyway. She wanted to go to a real school, and if she couldn't do that, she wanted to play outside. Why couldn't that rain stop?

"How about if I let you play Dress Up, with some old clothes from one of the trunks?" Mama asked.

"Dress Up!" cried Mary Elizabeth. She could speak very clearly now, but she still liked to mimic and repeat everything she heard.

Anna Rose liked the idea of playing Dress Up. They had never been allowed to open any of the trunks before. Mama took them to the attic and showed them which trunk they could take clothes from. It was not the trunk from Poland, but a shiny, black one. Mama opened it for them, and lifted out the top tray. A smell of moth balls wafted out and tickled Anna Rose's nose.

"You can play with any of the clothes you find in here," said Mama. "Try not to tear them."

"We won't," Anna Rose promised her.

Mama went back downstairs and the girls began to take out pieces of clothing. Virgie peered over the edge of the trunk. She was as curious to discover what was inside as her older sisters.

They lifted out a man's suit of dark blue wool. The jacket and trousers were enormous. They looked even bigger than the ones Daddy wore.

"These must have belonged to Grandpa Jake," said Anna Rose.

Next they lifted out a dark blue dress. There were shiny beads sewn on the front. They had never seen Mama wear this dress.

"It must have been Grandma's," guessed Anna Rose.

Below that was a gray dress of silvery, watery silk, with a white lace collar.

"I think Mama used to wear this." Anna Rose faintly remembered rubbing against the silky cloth as she sat in

Mama's lap. "I wonder why she doesn't wear it any more."

They found more older ladies' dresses. They each tried one on. Virgie did not want to put hers on. She only wanted to spread the skirt over herself and then pull it off. That was her way of playing peek-a-boo.

In the middle of the trunk were more men's suits. The trousers were shorter and very big at the waist. Anna Rose hoped they would find some hats and high-heeled shoes at the bottom. She wanted to walk around like a grand lady. But when they took out the last man's suit, a jumble of colorful cloth shone up at them. Something had red and white polka dots. Another piece, peeking through from the bottom, was covered with small spangles.

"What are these?" Anna Rose was almost breathless with excitement. She lifted out the red and white outfit. It was a clown suit, all in one piece, with big gathers at the ankles and wrists where tiny bells were sewn on. The matching cap had another bell attached to the end of the pointy tip. Holding it up against her, Anna Rose could see that it would almost fit. It would be only a little too big.

"These are children's costumes!" she gasped. Reaching in, she pulled out the next one. It was a dress with a blue skirt. Over the skirt was another skirt of blue and white flowered cloth that was gathered up in front and on the sides. There was a matching cap with ruffled elastic all around.

"It looks like the picture of Little Bo-Peep," cried Anna Rose.

"Little Bo-Peep has lost her sheep, and can't tell where to find them." Mary Elizabeth started to recite the Little Bo-Peep rhyme. She knew many Mother Goose rhymes by heart and, once she got started, would say them over and over.

Anna Rose was so excited, she did not know whether to stop and try on the Little Bo-Peep dress or take out the rest of the costumes. She decided to look at the others first. Maybe that would make Mary Elizabeth forget about the Little Bo-Peep rhyme. Already she had said it three times.

The cloth with the spangles lay at the very bottom of the trunk. On top of it was a brown and white dress with a square collar. Pinned to this were an apron and a plain white bonnet that had strings to tie under the chin. It was the kind of dress the Pilgrims wore at the first Thanksgiving. Anna Rose recognized it immediately from the pictures in the *Book Two Reader*.

At last the whole spangly dress could be seen. It was made of bright yellow, shiny material. And in the bottom corner of the trunk right next to it was a matching tall, pointed hat of the kind princesses wore in olden days. It had a veil that floated down behind, all the way to the floor. It was the most beautiful costume Anna Rose had ever seen. How could Mama have kept such treasures hidden at the bottom of a trunk all this time?

"Let's each put on a costume and go down to show Mama," suggested Anna Rose. She picked up the princess dress and started to slip it over her head.

"I want that one," said Janie, tugging at the princess dress.

"I saw it first. It's mine," insisted Anna Rose. She was supposed to share with her sisters, but she could not, no, she would not give up that princess dress. "You put on the Little Bo-Peep."

"Mary Elizabeth wants it." Janie kept tugging at the princess dress. "I want this one."

Anna Rose saw that Mary Elizabeth was struggling to

put the Little Bo-Peep dress over her head. She continued to recite the rhyme, for about the twentieth time.

"I just can't give up this dress," thought Anna Rose. She spied the tall, matching hat. It looked quite big. "Look," she said, as she placed the hat on Janie's head. "It's much too big for you. It comes down over your eyes. You put on the clown costume. It has all those jingly bells." Anna Rose transferred the hat to her head. It came down a little over her forehead. "See, this just fits me."

"Well, all right," grumbled Janie. "But I want to try that one after you." She pulled on the clown outfit and Anna Rose helped her slide the arms and legs up. The bells tinkled and jingled. Virgie looked up from where she was still playing hide-and-seek inside the skirt of the gray silk dress.

Quickly, Anna Rose tied the Pilgrim bonnet on Virgie's head. She did not want her crying for the clown suit, just because it had bells on it. They marched downstairs, holding up their skirts and pants legs.

115

"Mama, look what we found!"

"Where did these come from?"

"I'm Little Bo-Peep looking for her sheep."

As the girls all tried to speak at the same time, Mama stared at them in astonishment. Then she recovered with a laugh.

"For heaven's sake! Where did you find those?" she asked, but they could tell she knew the answer. For a moment, Mama's eyes had a faraway look. She was smiling to herself.

"Where did you get them?" Anna Rose repeated.

"Oh, a long time ago, when I was a girl, I earned some money and bought them," Mama answered dreamily.

"Was it before you lost your fingertip?" Anna Rose wanted to know. Mama's right pointing finger had no fingernail on it. The whole tip was missing. Sometimes she would tell them the story of when she was a naughty little girl, and how her fingertip got chopped off. Maybe she would tell them a story about the costumes.

"It was a few years after I lost my fingertip," laughed Mama. "I was already a pretty big girl."

"Tell us about it," begged Anna Rose.

Mama started remembering. "One time, in fall, my brothers decided to trap muskrats. There were a lot of them in the sloughs near our farm. They had read in the newspaper about a place in St. Louis where you could send muskrat skins and get a dollar for each one. I didn't think much of that until one day, I was visiting Grandma and Grandpa Guzinski. Aunt Pauline let me look at some of her fashion magazines and in one of them I saw an advertisement for some children's costumes. There was a picture of the costumes. 'Four for ten dollars,' it said. So, I asked my brothers to let me trap muskrats with them.

116

They didn't like it, but Ma said they had to. Finally, I had ten muskrat skins as my share. I sent them away and got my money in return, but the price had gone down and it wasn't quite enough. Ma could see I wanted those costumes, so she gave me the rest. I waited and waited. I thought that package would never come. At last it arrived. But when I opened it and tried them on, not one of them fit me. They were all too small. I looked at the advertisement again and, sure enough, in tiny print in the corner, it said 'For ages 6–9.' I didn't even have a little sister to try them on. That was a joke on me, wasn't it?" Mama finished with a smile.

Anna Rose did not think it was a joke. "I would have cried and cried," she thought. "Imagine, having those beautiful costumes and not being able to wear them."

"Can we play with them now?" the girls asked.

"All right. Just for today. But then I want you to put them away. In another year or two, they will just fit you. Then you can put on a little play for me. Don't forget to remind me about them."

"I won't forget." Anna Rose spoke in a sure voice. She was already planning pageants and plays in her imagination, and in every one, she was the princess.

First-Grade Hiccups

May was a busy month, as usual. Because Lawrence was not there, the others had to work extra hard to get all the chores done. Every day, when it was not raining, Mama worked in the garden. Anna Rose helped her, and at the same time kept an eye on the geese for Angie. Before long they would have to start chopping nettles. The last week of the month was also the last week of school.

"Wednesday is visiting day for the new first graders," Angie informed her mother. "Is Anna Rose coming with us?"

"She went to school with you one day last September. I don't think she needs to go again, do you?" Mama joked.

How could Mama tease about such an important thing? wondered Anna Rose. She just *had* to go! That was the day when she would meet all her new classmates and they would learn what was expected of them when they returned to school in the fall. She did not want to start school in September and sit there like a dummy, not knowing anyone and not sure how to act or what to do.

"I think she should go," Angie responded firmly. Anna Rose gave her a grateful glance. Sometimes older sisters could be very understanding.

Early Wednesday morning, they set off in the buggy. Next year, Francis would take the school bus to high school in Arcadia, but there was still no bus to pick them up and drive them to Pine Creek. Seven miles was a long way to walk, so they rode in the buggy, pulled by King and Dollie. Less than a mile down the main road, Francis stopped to pick up their two sets of cousins.

Anna Rose made room on the jump seat for her cousin Mary Ann who would be entering first grade with her. They were too excited to say much, so they watched the road instead. There were almost no cars coming or going in either direction. The farmers were busy working in the fields.

Francis pulled the team to a stop in front of the school and let them out. He had to stable the horses in Stencil's barn, farther down the road.

Angie took Anna Rose and Mary Ann by the hand and led them to the first- and second-grade room. In Pine Creek school, two or three grades always shared the same room and had the same teacher.

"This is Sister Teresianna." She introduced them to the teacher standing by the door. Sister Teresianna asked some children in the first row seats to move over. Usually, two children sat at each desk, but there was room on the bench for three if they squeezed together. The old first graders did not mind sitting so tightly cramped for one day. It was a sign they were almost ready for second grade. Besides, they could show off how much they knew about school.

The first half of the morning flew by. The new children learned how to answer "Present" when attendance was taken. They learned how to stand correctly and pledge allegiance to the flag. They learned to stand up in unison and say "Good morning, Sister Virginia," or "Good morning, Father Gara," when another teacher or the priest or a grown-up came into the room. They learned how to sharpen pencils, erase blackboards, and collect papers. In fact, there were so many things to learn and keep straight, Anna Rose was not sure she would remember them all until September.

During recess, they learned to play games that were different from those they played at home, like London Bridge and Run, Sheep, Run. Secretly, Anna Rose thought the games were silly and babyish. She already played older games like Ante, Ante, Over and Starlight, Moonlight.

After recess, they squeezed into the seats again. Sister Teresianna gave each of the old and new first graders a sheet with two rows of pictures.

"First-grade class, please show the new first graders how to color in the objects and then draw matching lines between the pictures that go together. I want you to work quietly while I hear the second grade recite their last reading lesson. If you must talk, do so in a whisper. You may spread out, two to a desk."

Sister directed the second-grade pupils to the circle of chairs in one corner of the classroom. She put one old first grader and one new one at each double desk. Anna Rose sat next to a boy named Stanley. She had heard the other boys call him Stash. He leaned over to explain what was written on the sheet.

"I can read it myself," whispered Anna Rose proudly. Silently, she read the instructions: "Color the pictures. Read the words. Draw a line between the pictures that go together. Example: Cup --------- Saucer." There was a long line between the picture of the cup and the picture of the saucer. She set to work, coloring each item carefully and then drawing the lines. She finished before Stanley had his sheet completed.

Anna Rose looked up. She was the first one finished. All the other first graders, old and new, were still hard at work, bent over their papers. In the corner, a second-grade boy was reading aloud. It was one of the last stories in the *Book Two Reader*. The boy stumbled over almost every word.

"I can read better than that!" bragged Anna Rose in a whisper.

"Bet you can't!" hissed Stanley back at her.

"I can, too." Anna Rose glanced up and saw that Sister Teresianna was looking in their direction. She signaled for a new pupil to begin reading and then silently strolled toward them.

Anna Rose froze in her seat. Had she done something wrong already? She wished she had not bragged to Stanley about knowing how to read. Without a word, Sister looked at her paper, smiled, and then returned to the reading group. Anna Rose sighed with relief.

Then she looked around. What was she supposed to do now? It was getting close to noon and she was hungry. She thought about the sandwiches and cookies in her lunch pail. Suddenly, she gave a big hiccup. It was so loud that the children sitting in the front rows turned around to look. Stanley was staring at her as if she were crazy or something.

"I can't help it," whispered Anna Rose, and just then another hiccup came out. It sounded like a short squeal. The children started to laugh. Anna Rose blushed. What an awful way to start school! She held her lips tight together and put her hands over them. Maybe if she sat quietly and held her breath the hiccups would go away.

Sister Teresianna heard the giggling of the first graders. She came to stand in front of the desks.

"What's the matter?" she asked Anna Rose. "Are you sick?"

Anna Rose was afraid to open her mouth to answer.

"Stand up and speak up!" urged Sister Teresianna.

Slowly, Anna Rose stood up. She dropped her hands and took a deep breath. "I have the . . . hicc!" Out of her mouth came the loudest hiccup she had ever heard. It sounded like an explosion. Even the second graders heard it, sitting way over in the corner. All the children tittered and snickered. Anna Rose felt she would melt with shame.

"Quiet everyone!" ordered Sister. "Stanley, take Anna Rose out to the water fountain. See if a good, long drink of water helps to stop those hiccups."

Meekly, Anna Rose followed Stanley out the door. She knew where the water fountain was, but she was afraid to open her mouth to say so. In the hallway, she took a long drink at the bubbling fountain.

"That was a good trick," said Stanley.

"It was not a trick. I really was hiccuping that way." Anna Rose was furious that he would think she could fool around on such an important day. "Just wait and see. They are probably not gone yet."

But no matter how long they waited, no more hiccups came. She was glad and sorry at the same time. Glad because she did not have to face all the stares of her new classmates as she hiccuped again. Sorry because she could not show Stanley how hard it was for her to get rid of the hiccups.

As they walked back into the classroom, the bell rang, announcing lunchtime. All the children were so hungry they forgot about the hiccups. Anna Rose fervently hoped they would not remember them during recess.

One or two of them made a fake hiccuping sound, but for the rest of the afternoon, none of the children had a moment to think about anything except the new games and the rules and regulations they were learning. Toward the end of the school day, Sister read aloud a story called "Toads and Diamonds." It was such a good story that even Anna Rose forgot about the hiccups. She could picture the diamonds and jewels pouring out of the mouth of the good girl and the snakes and toads spouting from the bad one.

The three o'clock bell pealed and the children scattered with whoops and hollers. Many of them had to walk home. A few got into cars that were waiting for them. The rest climbed into the buggies that waited in the barn.

All the way home, Anna Rose thought about the many things that had happened that day. She listened to the others in the buggy as they chatted about different events. She tried to recall all the details of the "Toads and Diamonds" story so that she could tell it to Janie and Mary Elizabeth. At last, she had started school. True, it was only for one day, and she had to wait for three more months to go every day. But she considered herself in first grade already.

That night, as she and her younger sisters were getting ready for bed, Anna Rose did not want to kneel down next to them.

"I want to say my prayers by myself, like Angie and Millie do," she protested. She thought it was babyish to have to kneel in a row and say each prayer out loud, slowly, so that even Virgie could follow the words.

"Be a good girl and lead your sisters," coaxed Mama.

"But you said as soon as I was in school I could say them by myself!"

"Yes, that's right. But you won't be in school until September. So kneel down, now, and start." Mama was firm and insistent.

"I am *too* in school! Sister Teresianna called us first

graders. She said she would see us *again* in September."

At first, Mama did not answer. Then she spoke again. "Well, did you pray silently in class, or did you pray out loud, together?" Anna Rose had to admit that they had prayed out loud, with Sister Teresianna leading them.

"It takes a long time to learn to pray by yourself," Mama said. "You can start in September. Until then, I want you to say your prayers out loud, with your sisters."

Anna Rose knelt next to Janie and started the "Our Father" in Polish. She rattled the words off without thinking about them. Instead, she was thinking of what an interesting day it had been in school. No matter what Mama said, she was a first grader.

Corn Rows

The June days were softly warm. Many nights there would be storms and rain, but when it was time for sunrise, the sky would be clear and pale blue.

"Things are growing so fast, I can't keep up with them," said Daddy. "I'll sure be glad when Lawrence gets back this week. Every row of corn needs cultivating. Those weeds like the good weather better than the corn."

"Don't forget the fields on the bottoms, Alex. I was down there today to take care of my melon plants. Those corn plants won't come to anything if they are not weeded soon." Mama was talking about the fields that lay right next to the railroad tracks and the river.

The ground of their farm was like five giant steps. Lowest of all was the part by the river. Then there was a

126

short steep hill to climb, and at the top a flat area for the barns, the house and gardens, the farmyard, and two small fields that sloped upward. The road made another level spot for the third step, with the biggest fields and meadows rising above it. Above the fields was another road, the one they took to go to the strawberry patch. It was the narrowest step of all. The highest step was the rocky bluff, with its sides planted in pine, hickory, oak and maple trees.

Anna Rose could picture a giant coming out of the swamp and climbing their stairstep farm: left foot on the bottom fields; right foot in the farmyard; left foot on the road; right foot on the upper road; left foot on the flat rocks of the bluff; right foot next to it. There he would stand, looking down at their farm on one side and the neighboring farms on the other sides.

While Anna Rose was imagining the giant stairsteps, Daddy was thinking about what to do with the corn in the lower fields. Finally he spoke to Francis.

"You had better hitch up Old Roan to the hand cultivator and see if that works. It may be too wet even for that. Come back if the cultivator starts pulling the plants up with the weeds."

Francis guided Old Roan down the steep hill. She was old and slow, but she was the best horse for cultivating. She always kept to a neat, straight line.

In less than an hour, Francis plodded with her, back up the hill. It was too wet, even for the hand cultivator. Daddy was busy out in another field, but Mama had an idea.

"You go out and help your Pa in the lower forty. I think Mildred and Anna Rose can start hoeing the corn by hand." Mama found two hoes with sharp edges. She handed them to the girls.

"Chop carefully around the corn stalks," she instructed them. "Try not to chop out too many corn plants. That would be such a help to us if you could get that one field weeded all by yourselves."

Anna Rose had never done this job before. She felt big and important, doing such grown-up work. Millie showed her how to chop out the thick, choking weeds from around the corn plants.

"You have to do it just right. If you chop too close, a stalk of corn will come out with the weeds; if you hoe too far away, you won't get all the weeds," Millie told her.

They hoed all morning. The rows seemed longer and longer. Anna Rose was just about to ask Millie if they could stop, when they heard a voice calling from the top of the hill overlooking the field: "Millie! Anna Rose! Time for dinner." Instead of walking around by the road, they climbed straight up the hill, walked through a short patch of bushy, tangly woods, and came out behind the granary. From there, it was only a hundred steps to the house.

"How is it going?" asked Mama as they sat down at the dinner table.

"Coming along. Coming along," replied Anna Rose, just like Lawrence always did, when things were going nicely.

Mama smiled and heaped their plates high with meat and potatoes and new leafy lettuce with sweet, thick cream dressing. Everyone ate twice as much as usual.

As soon as dinner was over, Millie and Anna Rose headed for the door. Mama stopped them.

"You don't have to go right back. Rest for a while yet."

Millie paused as if she wanted to stay, but Anna Rose

urged her on. "No, we want to get the field done today."

"All right, then," said Mama, "but I want you to carry along a pail of water and take a rest in the middle of the afternoon. I don't want you getting sunstroke."

Carrying a tin gallon pail of water, they worked their way through the brush and down to the field again. For a while, it was satisfying to hoe in silence. The tidy, straight rows of newly weeded corn contrasted pleasantly with the messy, frowzy rows in which the corn plants could hardly be seen. They were completely overgrown with crabgrass and all sorts of other weeds. The more they hoed, the nicer the field looked.

When they were both at the end of their rows, Millie stopped for a drink of water and Anna Rose joined her. They still had more than half the rows left to do, but for a while they rested under the shade of the trees at the edge of the field. It felt good to lie down instead of bending over. After a few minutes, Anna Rose jumped up.

"Let's race to see who can get a row done the fastest."

"Okay," agreed Millie.

Chop, chop, chop! Anna Rose hacked and slashed at the corn rows. In the row next to her, Millie did the same. They were going faster and faster.

"Oops!" cried Anna Rose as she chopped out half of a corn plant along with a big clump of crabgrass.

"I saw that," Millie taunted her. "It's not fair to hoe so fast you chop out the corn."

Anna Rose slowed down a little, but when she saw Millie getting ahead of her, she speeded up again. Chop, chop! Scratch, scrape! Millie hoed neatly and piled up the freshly turned earth so that it made a small hillock around each corn plant. She was being so careful that Anna Rose was now several feet ahead on her row. Millie quickened her pace. Chop! Rip! Her hoe lifted out an entire corn plant, roots and all, just as she was passing Anna Rose.

"That's one on you!" Anna Rose teased her. "Now there will be a space there."

Millie tried to replant the corn stalk but she was not sure it would live. It already looked a bit droopy.

Chop! Slash! Anna Rose looked down at the hillock of corn she had just finished. The entire corn plant was hacked off at the ground. It was not possible to replant it.

"Now there's one against you!" accused Millie.

They kept on hoeing fast.

"Two down for you!" cried Millie when she saw Anna Rose hack out another corn plant.

"And that's two down for *you*," Anna Rose twitted Millie in return, a few minutes later.

They continued their frenzied hoeing.

"Three for you!" shouted Millie. "And four for you!" she called out once more. "Ha, ha! I only have two down and you have four." But soon her hoe went off its mark again.

"Three for you!" triumphed Anna Rose.

They were almost at the end of their rows. Anna Rose glanced back and saw that these rows did not look nearly as neat and trim as those they had done earlier. Chopping around the last hillock, she saw that Millie was on her last plant, too. They finished in a tie.

"Maybe we better not race each other," suggested Anna Rose. She felt guilty. She had chopped down five whole corn plants, though Millie had only noticed four.

"Okay!" Millie sighed with relief.

The next rows they hoed at a slow and steady pace. Once more the hillocks looked just the way they should. They stopped again for a drink and a rest. There were quite a few rows still to be weeded, but their arms were getting stiff and tired.

No matter how careful they were now, they occasionally chopped out parts of some corn plants, but no more whole ones. When they heard Angie calling them from the top of the hill to come to supper, they were so glad they did not even care if they finished their rows.

"Well, how many hills of corn did you chop out?" Mama asked them teasingly.

"Oh, about four or five," mumbled Anna Rose. Millie was washing her face and hands at the sink, so she pretended not to hear and did not answer.

"What!" cried Mama, throwing up her hands in mock horror. "Was that whole plants or parts of plants?"

"It was whole plants," interrupted Millie. She did not want to tell Mama that she had chopped up plants, too. Neither did she want Mama to criticize their hard work. "We got almost the whole field done, and that's a lot of hoeing. There are only ten rows left," said Millie, defensively.

"Yes, you *were* hard workers today," agreed Mama. When Daddy came home, she told him what the girls had done. "Imagine, Alex, they weeded that whole field except for ten rows!"

"Jingers, crackers! This I have to see." Daddy did not come in to supper until after he went to the top of the hill and looked down at the cornfield. He came back beaming with pleasure. "I never would have believed it until I saw it," he said. "Why, I would have said that field needed two or three days of work, for sure, to get all that quack grass out."

Anna Rose and Millie blushed with pride. If Daddy said that, it meant they had done a good job. Tomorrow they would finish it.

Strawberry Surprise

"Those CCC workers sure did a good job," said Daddy as the family drove home from church one Sunday. He was looking up at the rows and rows of small pine trees stretching almost to the top of the big bluff that hid their farm from the main road.

"What does CCC mean?" asked Anna Rose.

"Civilian Conservation Corps," Francis sounded out the words distinctly and importantly. He wanted to show how smart he was. "Those are men who can't get any other jobs so the government gives them work. They planted those trees a couple of years ago."

"Well, I can tell you I'm not joining any CCC, now that I know mechanics and welding," bragged Lawrence.

He had just come back from a special course in Winona. "I'm going off to work in a big city, as soon as I get a job."

Mama and Daddy were silent. They did not want Lawrence to go, but he was determined to leave the farm. For a moment, no one in the car spoke. When they came to the foot of the hill, Daddy turned the car off to the left instead of continuing on down the main road.

"Where are you going, Alex?" Mama asked in alarm. This was a bumpy road, more like a wagon track.

"To check on the strawberries," laughed Daddy.

"Oh, I don't think we'll get many berries this year," Mama replied doubtfully. "We planted them so late, and it really takes two years before there is a good crop."

Daddy stopped the car. He could not go all the way to the strawberry patch so he walked up to the edge of it. He ruffled the plants back and forth. Everyone could see him pop a berry into his mouth.

"There *are* some berries. I think you might get one good picking," said Daddy when he returned to the car.

"I'll go," offered Lawrence. He loved strawberries as much as the others did. Maybe more.

"First you will all go home and change your clothes," insisted Mama. "Besides, we have no boxes or pails in the car."

Daddy turned the car around and went back to the road that led to their front gate. The moment they were in the house, the older children ran upstairs to change into old clothes. Anna Rose went, too.

"It's a long ways, you know, and we have to walk. Can you keep up with us?" asked Angie.

"What do you think?" Anna Rose was disgusted. "I'm not a baby any more. I'll be going to school this fall, remember?"

"Okay, okay! You can come," agreed Angie. "I just thought I would warn you."

After eating some snails and drinking some milk they set off, swinging tin gallon pails in their hands. It *was* a long way. By the time they got to the patch, Anna Rose was hungry and thirsty again. She wished she had eaten another snail and drunk another glass of milk.

"Let's each take a row and see who gets the most," suggested Lawrence. Bending low, they began to push the strawberry leaves from side to side, searching for the ripe, red berries. After ten minutes of searching, Anna Rose had found only eight.

"Ma was right," called out Francis. "There are hardly any berries. I don't even see many green ones."

"Just keep on picking," insisted Lawrence. "Maybe at the other end of the rows there will be more."

But when they had finished all the rows, they each had only about two inches of berries in their pails. Enough to cover the bottom.

"If we put them all in one pail, it would be three quarters full," said Angie hopefully.

Lawrence had a gleam in his eyes. He was thinking up some mischief, they could see that.

"Let's put grass in the bottom of our pails, and then strawberries on top. That way, we will fool them and make them believe we picked five gallons." Lawrence's eyes glowed as he emptied his berries into Anna Rose's pail. He started to pull grass from the edge of the field.

"I think we should put them all in one pail," Angie said with hesitation.

"Aw, shucks, can't we have a little fun?" Lawrence coaxed her. It did not take long for Angie to change her mind. They pulled grass until there was enough to fill

135

each pail three-quarters full. Carefully, they divided the berries and spread them over the top of the grass, until it was no longer visible in any of the pails. Each pail looked as though it were plump full of ripe, red berries. Then, singing and laughing, the pickers walked back to the house.

Daddy was sitting on the front porch, relaxing and smoking his pipe. "Jingers, crackers! You really did get a lot of berries," he exclaimed.

"Oh, we got quite a few," answered Lawrence innocently.

Mama heard the commotion and came out from the kitchen. She had started dinner and things were already beginning to smell good.

"Well, look at that!" Mama was almost speechless with surprise. "I can't believe you found so many berries!" After a bit, she recovered and had an idea: "I'll make some shortcake right now. Angeline, you tend to the chicken, while I stir it up."

Angie was going to say something but Lawrence pushed her into the kitchen. Mama followed her and took out a big bowl; she mixed flour, baking powder, and lard with her fingers. Then she added a little sugar and a pinch of salt. She poured in enough milk to make the dough stick together, and plopped it in neat mounds on two baking sheets. As soon as she had popped the shortcakes into the oven, she turned to the pails of berries.

"Somebody will have to help me wash and hull them," said Mama. "Bring me the colander, Anna Rose." Then Mama noticed that the boys and Millie were standing around, watching her.

"What's the matter?" asked Mama. "Can't you wait until dinner for your strawberries?" They grinned back at her.

Shake, shake! Mama gently shook the berries from one pail into the colander. After a moment, grass began to fall out.

"Who picked grass instead of berries? Was that you, Anna Rose?" Mama still had not caught on that the rest of the pail was full of grass. Francis snickered and Millie giggled. Mama looked inside the pail. She pushed her hand to the bottom. All she could feel was grass. With a suspicious look at Lawrence, she picked up another pail. This time she took it carefully, letting only the strawberries fall into the colander. She was watching for the grass. Without a word, she did the same to the other three pails. The children were giggling and grinning.

"You rascals, you!" cried Mama. "Making me think there were so many berries. And I was right all along. I'll bet there isn't even one pailful." Mama turned her back on them and heaved her shoulders as though she were crying.

"Aw, Ma, we just wanted to tease you," said Lawrence.

"Well, you'll get what's coming to you," answered Mama as she turned around. They could see now she was laughing, not crying. "You clean every blade of grass out of these berries and then hull them and wash them," she ordered. "Maybe we'll have enough for one round of shortcake."

Lawrence and Francis and Anna Rose started picking out the grass while Millie set the table and did other things for Mama. It was tedious picking out the slender spikes of grass which clung to the berries as though they were glued. It took them a long time to get the berries hulled and clean. The rest of the family sat down to eat before they were finished. Mama got up to sugar the berries and set them aside in the pantry, next to the shortcakes that were cooling on a rack. Lawrence and Francis and Anna Rose rushed to the table.

They ate swiftly, eagerly looking forward to dessert. As soon as all their plates were clean, Mama went to the pantry. She carne out with a big portion of shortcake, smothered with strawberries and whipped cream. She put it in front of Daddy. In front of Janie and Mary Elizabeth she put smaller portions, with the shortcake crumbled into tiny pieces. Virgie got a small dish of strawberries with a little cream. Then Mama came back with another large portion. She sat down and began to eat it.

The older children sat there, their mouths drooling, but not saying a word. At last, Anna Rose could stand it no longer.

"Don't we get any shortcake?"

"Yes," put in Lawrence, "what about us? After all, we picked the berries."

Mama laughed. "I was only teasing you," she mimicked Lawrence. "All right, Angeline, you can go and dish out the rest of the shortcake and berries. Mind that you give equal portions."

Finally, they could dig into the luscious strawberry shortcake. The sweetened berries and soft whipped cream tasted just right with the crunchy shortcake.

"Mm, mmm," cried Lawrence, "nothing tastes better than the first strawberries of summer. I only wish we *had* gotten five pails full."

The Grapevine Swings

During the first days of July, Anna Rose and Millie and
Angie hoed the corn in the other bottom field. This field
was twice as big as the one they had already hoed and the
ground was even wetter. The corn was short and puny
looking because Daddy had planted it two weeks later
than the other fields.

One afternoon, Lawrence said he would come and
help them. As they walked down the steep hill, he noticed
the wild grapevines hanging from the trees lining the dirt
roadway. He grabbed hold of one of the thick vines,
stepped backward a few paces, took a running jump, and
swung out over the hill's edge.

"Woo-woo-woo-woo!" he trumpeted. "I'm Tarzan of

the jungle!" He swung out, back and forth, at least six times. Then he dropped back onto the edge of the road.

"I want to do that!" cried Anna Rose. It looked like fun.

"No, don't you dare try it. That's too dangerous for little girls." Lawrence was serious for a change. He had a guilty look on his face. "I should never have done that. You forget all about it," he urged.

But Anna Rose could not forget about the vines. Every day as they walked past, she eyed them longingly. It had seemed to be like flying, the way Lawrence swung out over the ravine at the edge of the hill.

When the corn in the bottom field was finished, there was not as much work for them to do. Anna Rose could play all day, every day. Most of the time she liked playing with her sisters, but now, she wanted to play by herself. She was going to try swinging on the grapevines when no one was looking.

One afternoon she slipped away and ran to the hill. The grapevines hung in thick, ropy strands from most of the trees along the upper edge of the roadway. Anna Rose selected a sturdy vine. She tested it by hanging on with all her weight and lifting her feet off the ground. The vine held her up with no sign of breaking.

Cautiously, Anna Rose gave herself a gentle push with her feet. She swung out a few feet over the ravine. She pushed a little harder and this time swayed out almost ten feet. Below her, she could see a deeper part of the ravine. She felt a tickling in her belly. It was as much fun as she had thought it would be. She was just about to push herself even farther out when she heard Janie's voice calling from the top of the roadway.

Like a shot, Anna Rose dropped back to the ground, let go of the vine, and ran to meet Janie.

"What are you doing down there?" asked Janie suspiciously. She did not like to be left out of things.

"Nothing," replied Anna Rose. Secretively, she looked back to see if the vines were shaking or swinging. They were moving a little, as though a breeze were blowing. It was not enough to give her away.

"I want you to play with me," begged Janie.

"All right." Anna Rose agreed immediately. For the rest of that day she played with Janie and Mary Elizabeth. But every day after that, she tried to slip away from them, when no one else was looking, either. She could not keep away from the vines.

One day, Anna Rose was gliding smoothly, back and forth, over the edge, over the roadway, over the ravine, over the roadway, over the deeper ravine, over the roadway.

"What are you doing?" Janie's voice sounded right at her back. Anna Rose jumped so hard she almost let go of the vine before her feet were safely over the roadway.

"What are you doing?" echoed Mary Elizabeth. She had tagged along with Janie.

"Oh, no!" thought Anna Rose. "Now they have both seen me. What am I going to do?" She stared at her sisters. They stared back at her.

"I want to try swinging like that," said Janie, reaching for one of the vines.

"Uh, ummm," Anna Rose hesitated, trying to think of something to say. If she said "You can't," that would be the worst, because then Janie would want to swing all the more. Finally, she told Janie: "I was just trying it out but it's no fun. Let's go swing on the real swing."

"I want to swing here," insisted Janie, and without another word she grasped one of the vines tightly, took a running leap, and sailed out over the ravine. She caught on right away, how to push herself with her feet. Soon she was swaying out over the deepest part of the ravine, farther than Anna Rose had dared to go.

"This is fun," she called out. Anna Rose watched the vine anxiously. It seemed to be holding well. Janie was pretty skinny. Maybe she weighed the same as several big bunches of grapes. After all, if the vines did not fall down when the grapes were hanging on them, they should be able to hold up a skinny little girl. Anna Rose was trying to convince herself that this was true, when Mary Elizabeth called out: "I want to swing."

"Oh, no. You can't. You are not three years old yet," Anna Rose told her firmly. Fortunately, Mary Elizabeth didn't argue. There were so many things she was not allowed to do or had to wait for. People were always saying to her: "Wait till you are three years old, in September."

Anna Rose watched Janie sailing happily back and forth.

"You stop for a while and watch Mary Elizabeth. Now it's my turn to swing," she called.

"You said it was no fun," answered Janie.

"But I wasn't swinging out that far," argued Anna Rose. Janie swayed to and fro a few more times and then stopped. Anna Rose took hold of the vine and pumped herself out. Now she was flying as far over the ravine as Janie had. It was scary and exciting. She took one quick look down. The deep green ferns on the banks of the ravine were so hidden in shadow, they seemed almost black. Suddenly, Anna Rose did not like it so much any more. She felt as though the darkness at the bottom of the ravine were pulling her down. She dropped her feet and fell with a tumble, onto the roadway.

"What's the matter?" asked Janie.

"I don't want to swing any more," was all Anna Rose would say.

"Well, I do. I'm going to try it one more time." Janie took off again, pushing herself harder and harder. All at once, Anna Rose heard a loud snapping noise, just as Janie reached the point over the deepest part of the ravine. She darted her eyes up to where the vine twined around a fat tree branch and screamed in horror.

"Come back! The vine is breaking."

The momentum of the swing brought Janie halfway back, but at that point the vine gave way completely and Janie dropped, down, down, halfway down the deep ravine.

Anna Rose stood stock-still in terror. She peered down at Janie, lying flat on her back in a patch of ferns. Janie was not moving. At last, Anna Rose found her voice.

"Run to Mama!" she urged Mary Elizabeth. "Tell her to come quick. Maybe Janie is dying."

Mary Elizabeth turned and ran. As soon as she got halfway across the farmyard, Anna Rose could hear her shrieking: "Mama, Mama! Come quick! Janie's dying, Janie's dying!"

With trembling knees, Anna Rose climbed down the ravine to where Janie lay. She looked at her closely. She was not moving a muscle.

"Oh, no!" sobbed Anna Rose. "She really is dying." She remembered the times when she was mad at Janie, or jealous, and wanted to push her. Once or twice she had even thought to herself: "What if Janie were dead? Then people would pay attention to me." But now Anna Rose discovered she did not want Janie to die. She wanted her to live, so they could play together and be sisters.

"Oh, please stay alive," begged Anna Rose. Then she realized that Janie could not hear her. "I'll pray, that's what. God can hear me." Anna Rose started saying aloud the first prayer that came into her head. Halfway through, she stopped. She was saying the prayer they used before meals. "How can I be so dumb?" she thought, and sobbed all the harder. No other prayers came to her tongue. "Oh, God! Oh, God!" was all she could say.

"I'm coming, I'm coming!" She heard Mama call from the top of the roadway. The sound of Mama's voice released something inside of her. She heard herself starting the "Our Father." Now she remembered all the prayers they said every night, even the one about the guardian angel. She was saying it aloud as Mama came

145

stumbling down and leaned over Janie, listening to her heart and holding her wrist.

"Thanks be to God, she's alive," exclaimed Mama. She repeated it over and over again.

In a few moments, Janie's eyelids began to twitch. She groaned a little.

"Lie still. I'm here," Mama calmed her, stroking her head.

Janie groaned louder. She opened her eyes. "Where am I?" she asked with a puzzled look.

"Lie still for a minute," Mama told her. She lifted up one of Janie's legs and then the other. "Does that hurt?" she asked. Janie shook her head "No." Mama did the same thing with her arms. They seemed to be all right, too. "Now, lift your head a little and move it side to side." Mama held her arm under Janie's neck as Janie raised her head a few inches. Then, Mama lifted Janie in her arms and started to carry her up to the roadway.

"Does it hurt anywhere?" asked Mama again, anxiously.

"In my head, a little," answered Janie.

Slowly, they walked to the house and Mama put Janie to bed. She watched her all afternoon. When suppertime came, Mama told Daddy what had happened. She called them "naughty girls," but she never did scold them outright. Anna Rose thought she would get a spanking, but she did not.

The next day, Janie was fine. Her head did not hurt any more. They went to the roadway to look again at the place where she had fallen. But they did not swing on the vines. Not that day, or ever again.

The Tornado

"I have never seen such a streak of good summer weather," exclaimed Mama. "It's bound to break one of these days."

During all of July they had fine days. There was just enough rain to keep things growing well. Mostly it rained at night or in the early morning hours.

The corn started to tassel in the middle of July. The second crop of hay was growing taller and thicker than ever before. The oats fields rippled with the slender but sturdy stalks, lightly bending their heads under the weight of their golden pockets of grain.

"Some of those acres will give us sixty bushels, if this keeps up," said Daddy in hopeful anticipation. "We might have extra to sell." Most of the oats was ground up and fed to the cows, along with hay and corn silage.

"Don't count your chickens before they are hatched, Alex." Mama did not want Daddy to brag about the oats until it was all threshed.

Daddy and the boys worked extra hard in the fields, keeping up with all the growing things. They had their supper late every night, and went to bed right after eating.

Early one morning, before it was light, Anna Rose was awakened by the noise of a storm. The crackles of lightning and the booming of thunder sounded much like other storms they had had. But there was something different about this one. Anna Rose was wondering what it could be when she heard Angie's whisper: "Come downstairs."

Angie picked up Mary Elizabeth, who was sound asleep. Janie was rubbing her eyes and yawning.

"Mama said you are supposed to come downstairs," repeated Angie.

They felt their way down the silent, dark stairwell, not saying a word. When they got to the bottom, Angie turned toward the front room and Anna Rose and Janie followed. In the light of several flickering candles, Anna Rose could see that Millie was already there, and so were Lawrence and Francis.

Angie set Mary Elizabeth, still sleeping, down on the couch. Janie and Anna Rose perched on the edge of it, in front of her. The others sat on the sofa or on chairs, but Mama paced back and forth across the room, fingering her rosary.

"Why did we have to come downstairs?" Anna Rose wondered. She wanted to ask Mama, but she knew Mama did not like to be interrupted when she was praying.

They sat quietly, listening to the storm. Suddenly, Anna Rose realized what was different this time. It was the wind. Usually the doors and windows rattled and creaked as the wind buffeted them in and out. Now, there was the sound of a steady, high-pitched hum. The wind was blowing hard and fast, without a pause, and always in one direction, instead of puffing and huffing here and there, first one way and then another.

"Is this a tornado?" asked Anna Rose in a soft whisper. No one answered her. Once or twice every summer, during storms that were especially strong, Mama made them all go down in the cellar.

"It might be a tornado," she always said.

Secretly, Anna Rose had always wished she could stay upstairs and look out the windows. She wanted to see what a tornado looked like. On the radio, when they talked about tornadoes, they always mentioned a funnel touching down to the ground. Mama had a small funnel that she used when filling up jars. Daddy had a big funnel to pour gas into the tractor and truck. Anna Rose tried to imagine such a funnel, so gigantic that it filled the sky. Did the wind come down through the hole in the bottom of the funnel? she wondered.

"Is this a tornado?" Anna Rose repeated her question in a louder whisper.

"Hush!" replied Angie. "Yes, it probably is."

"How come we don't go down to the cellar?" asked Anna Rose.

"Because it came up too fast. We would get blown away now if we tried to go around the back of the house to the cellar." Angie explained it so clearly that Anna Rose could picture them all being blown about like the feathers they had stripped. Now that she knew there was a tornado outside, she wanted to see it. She edged to the window and peeked out. All she could see was a stream of raindrops sliding slantwise across the windowpanes.

"Come away from the window, quickly!" Mama snatched her arm and pulled her back to the couch. "Sit quietly, now, and pray." Mama spoke in a worried voice.

Anna Rose tried to say some prayers inside her head, but she kept thinking about the tornado. What if the giant funnel came right over their heads? Could the wind blow their house down, or suck it up the funnel? No, such a thing could never happen, of that she was sure. Their house was made of heavy stones and plaster. It was like the house of the third little pig: it would never get blown down.

"Where is Daddy?" With her question, Janie interrupted Anna Rose's thoughts and Mama's pacing.

"He's sleeping," Mama reassured them. "He needs his rest. We can wake him if we need him."

The wind began to hum louder, in a deeper tone. Every now and then they could hear a tree branch crack and fall. Sometimes the branches brushed against the house, scraping and scratching.

"I should be scared, but I'm not," thought Anna Rose. She felt so safe and snug in their stone house, with Mama praying and the candles flickering.

Soon the wind was so loud they could hear nothing else. It sounded like a train going by, only instead of coming from far down the hill, on the railroad tracks, it seemed to be right outside their house.

Craaaaaaack! Something split and tore apart. They jumped.

"That was scary," said Anna Rose, but no one could hear her.

Mama crossed herself and breathed a prayer. Lawrence stood a few feet from the window and tried to peer out.

"The barn is still standing," he said quietly. "It must have been one of the sheds at the back."

Finally, they could hear the wind begin to let up. Every minute the moaning and whistling got lower and fainter. After ten minutes, there was only the sound of the rain, and soft rumblings of thunder moving off into the distance.

"No sense going back to bed," announced Lawrence. "It's almost milking time anyway." He and Francis went upstairs to get dressed.

"You can go back to bed for a while," Mama told the girls. They filed back upstairs. Angie carried Mary Elizabeth. She had slept through it all. The clouds were breaking apart and a pale dawn light shone through. The girls heard Francis and Lawrence clumping down the stairs. From the kitchen came muffled noises as Mama started to light a fire in the stove.

"I'm not sleepy any more," said Anna Rose.

"Me neither," agreed Janie.

They peeked into the bedroom next to them and saw Angie and Millie getting dressed.

"If they can get dressed, we can, too," said Anna Rose. She wanted to go out as soon as the rain stopped, to see what had cracked and tumbled down during the tornado.

They waited while Mama made breakfast. The light in the windows got stronger and brighter. The rain was just a light patter on the panes now, and by the time they finished eating, it had stopped entirely. The sun came shining over the rim of the bluff.

"Can we go out and look around?" asked Angie.

"All right." Mama nodded her consent. "Just be sure you don't go too close to any trees or buildings that look as though they might topple down. I'll be out soon myself to see the damage."

They traipsed out in their bare feet. The puddles felt deliciously cool. In the front yard were dozens of small tree branches and twigs. Anna Rose gazed over the farmyard, her glance sweeping from the barn to the granary and corncrib, to the toolshed, and back to the barn. It was standing solid and firm and red as usual.

"Something doesn't look right about the barn." Anna Rose turned to Angie as she spoke.

"The cupola is missing!" gasped Angie.

Swiftly, Anna Rose glanced up to the top peak of the barn. A small hole, surrounded by an outline of ripped-off planks, showed where the cupola once had been. It had

sat on the top of the roof like a tiny house.

"So that's what made the cracking noise," said Anna Rose. She followed Angie, who was hurrying to the other side of the barn to see where the cupola had landed.

"It's not here!" cried Angie in surprise as they turned the corner and surveyed the yard on the far side of the barn. They ran to the edge of the farmyard, where a line of trees hid one of the fields. They climbed up on the gate by the road and scanned the fields as far as they could. The cupola was nowhere in sight.

Back they ran to the house, to tell Mama what they had discovered. Daddy was sitting at the kitchen table, eating bread and butter and drinking his coffee.

"The cupola blew off the barn," Angie told him excitedly, "but it's not on the ground anywhere near. It must have been blown far away."

"We'll be lucky if that's all the damage there is." Daddy sounded discouraged. As soon as he had finished breakfast, he went out to the barn and checked the other buildings as well. Nothing else seemed to be missing.

"We might as well have a look at the fields right away, too." Daddy's voice seemed to be saying he did not really want to go.

"What could the tornado do to the fields?" asked Anna Rose.

"Come along and you'll see," invited Daddy. The girls followed him up to the gate and along the road. As soon as they came near the oats field, Anna Rose could see what Daddy had feared. The stalks were not standing up in straight, rippling rows. Instead, swaths of flattened oats weaved in and out over the field. It was as though a giant barrel had rolled in twisting turns, up and down the field. Now the oats would be hard to harvest.

When they came to the cornfields, it was much the same. The tall, sturdy stalks were still standing in many places, but in others they were flattened down or tilting sideways, with their pulled-up roots showing.

"Is it bad?" Mama asked when they returned to the farmyard.

"Not as bad as I expected," answered Daddy. "We'll be able to harvest more than half of it. With a week or two of good sunshine, more of the oats might spring back. We'll see. But we didn't find the cupola."

Later that morning, Uncle Roman drove into the yard.

"Are you all safe and sound?" he asked.

"Yes, thanks be to God," replied Mama. "We seem to have lost the cupola from the barn, that's all. Alex says the fields aren't too bad, considering."

"Say, I think I know where the cupola landed." Uncle Roman's face lit up. "Leola Busse, your neighbor down the road, said a small shed landed in their front field. They didn't know where it came from."

The next day, the Winona newspaper showed a picture of the tornado on the front page. It was fuzzy and dark, but Anna Rose could make out a funnel-like shape. The article told about all the damage that had been done. Mama read it aloud while they looked over her shoulder.

. . . Several farms in the Dodge area had small sheds or buildings swept away. One farmer lost the cupola off the top of his barn. It was found in a field three miles distant . . .

"Why, that must be us," interrupted Anna Rose. She listened as Mama read the rest of the article.

"I'm glad we weren't outside during that tornado," commented Millie.

"Somebody must have been," retorted Anna Rose. "Otherwise, how could they take the picture?"

"Just be glad it wasn't you," Mama sighed with relief.

"Some day, I hope they make a building with a big, strong window where you can look out and see a tornado," said Anna Rose wishfully.

Millie was doubtful that would work. "It would be raining so hard you still couldn't see."

"It could have windshield wipers to help keep the rain away," insisted Anna Rose.

"Well, I for one hope I never come close enough to see a tornado." Mama was shaking her head at Anna Rose's idea. "When you grow up, you will probably feel the same."

Anna Rose did not agree. She was sure that she would always want to see a tornado, as long as she could be safe inside, with the candles burning and Mama praying.

Scarecrow in the Hay

"Time to start the second crop of hay," said Daddy. It was another fine day in August. For two whole days, he and Lawrence mowed hay, taking turns. They let it dry a day or two and then it had to be raked over to dry on the other side.

"The hay on the far field is dry now," Daddy informed them one day at the dinner table. "We'll start bringing it in this afternoon."

"Oh, Alex, I was going to start cutting out the girls' new dresses this afternoon." Mama did not usually complain, but she had her plans made for the afternoon, and now she would have to change them. It was Mama who usually drove the horses or tractor that pulled the wagon and the hay-loader.

"I don't think you need to come. Angie can take over, can't you, Angie?"

"Sure. I can do it." Angie stood up tall.

"Can I go with you?" asked Anna Rose.

"Why don't you wait for an hour or so and then you and Millie bring us water," suggested Lawrence. "We're using both wagons. That will take some time to load. It gets hot out there."

Daddy attached one wagon to the tractor, and backed it up to the hay-loader. Lawrence hitched Birdie and Sal to the other wagon and they set off for the field.

"I want to carry some water to the field," said Janie. "I want to ride on the top of the haywagon."

"I want to ride on the hay," piped up Mary Elizabeth.

"It's too far for you to walk in this hot sun," said Mama. "You can both meet the wagon at the gate, and ride down from there."

After waiting more than an hour, Anna Rose and Millie filled two tin pails with water. They plopped a chunk of ice into each. It took them almost half an hour to walk out to the far field. By the time they got there, the ice had melted, but the water was still cold.

One of the wagons was now stacked full of hay. It stood off to the side. Anna Rose watched as Angie guided the horses over a row of cut hay, one horse on each side of the row. Behind that came Daddy and Francis in the wagon. They were spreading the hay evenly as it came off the hay-loader in clumps. Lawrence walked behind the hay-loader, making sure it picked up all the hay. If any was left behind, he forked it up to the wagon.

Anna Rose and Millie watched the smooth movements of the horses, plodding along at an even, steady speed. Daddy and the boys knew just when to reach out with their pitchforks, lifting and spreading the hay to all corners of the wagon. They came to the end of a row and stopped for a drink.

"Ahhhhh! That tastes good." Daddy drank right from the pail, letting some water splash onto his face.

"Francis, you can take that full wagon back to the barn. It shouldn't be long before we fill this one. I can do the spreading myself."

Anna Rose eyed the tall mound of hay heaped onto the full wagon.

"Want to go up there?" asked Lawrence. He swung her up to the side of the wagon, where she grabbed hold of the slats. "Now, climb. I'll give your feet a push." Anna Rose grabbed at the hay and inched upward. Lawrence gave her feet a push and—plump! She landed at the top. Soon Millie had scrambled up beside her. Now they were on top of the world, it seemed. They were higher than Daddy, higher than some of the trees at the edge of the road. Anna Rose lay flat on her stomach and peeked over the side. It was such a long way down to the ground. She

and Millie sat in the sweet-smelling hay and gazed at everything as they went by. It all looked so different from up high.

Francis drove slowly. They liked it when he came to a bump or a dip in the road. It made them bounce and jiggle. Soon they came to the gate. There were Janie and Mary Elizabeth, waiting for their ride. Francis stopped the tractor.

"I want to go way to the top," said Janie.

"Okay! Grab hold while I give you a push." Francis placed one hand under each of Janie's feet and pushed hard.

"Yippee!" cried Janie as she somersaulted over the edge and landed in the center of the hayload.

"Catch hold of Mary Elizabeth's hands," Francis told Millie.

"I can climb by myself," protested Mary Elizabeth, and before Millie could reach out to her, she scrambled up like a monkey and tumbled to the top.

"Are you ready?" called Francis. He started the tractor with a jerk. The girls shrieked and held onto each other. All the way down to the barn, the tractor jerked and coughed.

"You are doing that on purpose," accused Anna Rose.

"Honest, I'm not," answered Francis. "I can't get this clutch in the right spot."

They hollered and squeaked and squealed with each jerk, but it was not really dangerous. They were safe in a rounded-out hollow, in the center of the load.

"We're birds in a nest," called out Anna Rose. She stood up and waved her arms. Jerk! She was thrown back down in her "nest," giggling and laughing. Francis pulled the load of hay close to the barn and stopped the tractor.

"Would you birdies like to fly down from there?" he asked. He held out his arms and waited at the side of the wagon.

"Okay, here comes the first bird!" shouted Millie. She put Mary Elizabeth at the edge of the load, and gave her a little shove.

Wheeeee! Down the side slid Mary Elizabeth, right into Francis's arms.

"Now me!" cried Janie, and down she flew.

At last it was Anna Rose's turn. The moment before she slid, she almost got scared and said she would climb down but by then it was too late. Down, down the slippery hay she glided, in one swooping motion. Francis was there to catch her so she did not land too hard.

"Let's do it again," begged Anna Rose.

"Oh, no. Once is enough for each load," protested Francis. "Wait up at the gate for the next one. They might give you another ride."

The girls hurried back up to the gate and waited impatiently for the other load to appear. At last, they saw it pull up over the small incline. When it reached the gate, Lawrence helped them up to the top. Once more they scrambled for the best place to survey the world. All too soon they pulled up at the barn.

"We're little birds, learning to fly," called out Anna Rose. "Catch us, Lawrence." Down they all slid again, into his arms.

It took almost an hour to unload the hay from the wagons. When they were finished, Mama brought out some cookies and a tall pitcher of lemonade.

"We have time for two more loads if you start the chores and milking," Daddy appealed to Mama.

"Well, I guess so," agreed Mama. "I got most of the dress pieces cut out."

This time, Anna Rose and Millie could not go out to the field. They had to help Mama prepare for milking and do some of the chores. First the cows had to be brought in from the pasture. Then there were pigs to feed, and chickens and geese. After all this was done, Mama started milking. They watched for a while.

"If you go up to the gate to watch for the loads, take Virginia with you, but watch her carefully," cautioned Mama.

Arriving at the gate, they saw they were just in time. Coming down the road was Francis with the first load.

"Are you coming for your first hayride?" Francis asked Virgie.

"Da," answered Virgie. It was her favorite word, of the three or four she could say. Francis swung her up carefully while Anna Rose reached out and pulled her to the top. Right away, Virgie started to crawl to the edge.

"Oh, no. I'm holding you in my lap," said Anna Rose. Virgie squealed and squirmed. She wanted to go on exploring the hay.

In front of the barn, they glided down once more, with Francis waiting below to stop them from falling.

"I'm a barn swallow," decided Anna Rose as she swooped down the side of the hayrack. The swallows made swoops and dives as they darted in and around the barn.

The last load arrived and they had their final slide for the day. It was already dusky outside. The sun was a round orange ball, glowing through the trees on the hill above the river.

"We'll have to hurry to get this all in the haymow before dark," said Daddy.

"Pa, can't we wait till morning to put it in?" pleaded Lawrence.

"I'm not taking a chance. We had so many night storms this year." Daddy was insistent.

Grumbling a little, Lawrence and Francis climbed up into the haymow. Angie hitched the horses to the rope and pulley. Daddy stood on the loaded wagon, on top of the hay. He pulled the rope, twitched it until the hooked fork left the track, and watched carefully as it descended. With his end of the rope, Daddy guided the fork so it landed in the middle of the load of hay. Pulling a lever, he made the hooks straighten out downward, forming a sharp, pointy fork. Then he pushed the fork deep down into the hay, standing on it to make sure it was as deep as it could go. Once more he pulled the lever and Anna Rose knew that the hooks were opened outwards again, underneath a thick layer of hay.

"All set," Daddy called to Angie.

"Giddyap," she clucked to the horses. The team tugged at the rope and slowly, slowly, a huge bundle of hay began to rise from the wagon. Higher and higher it rose until it came to the big doorway set into the upper side of the barn, under the eaves. Click! It reached the track in the ceiling and rolled smoothly along. As soon as it reached the back of the haymow where Lawrence and Francis were standing, they called out, "Stop!"

Daddy pulled the trip wire, making the hooks straight. The hay was flung down and the boys quickly scattered it with pitchforks. They had to spread it evenly, over the entire haymow, before the next big bundle was dropped down. It was hard work. They could not run fast on the soft hay. Once in a while, their feet hit a pocket of empty space under a thin layer of hay and down they would sink, up to their knees or higher. They had to be careful not to fall on their pitchforks.

The last curve of the sun slipped down through the trees. The light faded. It grew darker.

"I can't see a thing up here," complained Lawrence loudly.

"Anna Rose, climb up to that opening there and call out to them and to me when the fork is ready to release," Daddy ordered.

She entered the barn, climbed up the ladder to the hayloft and walked to the front part, where a small doorway was cut out of the side of the barn. It seemed a funny place for a door. If you stepped out, you would go tumbling more than twenty feet to the ground.

"Now I see what it's for," exclaimed Anna Rose as she sat down by the doorway. She could see everything that was happening outside, and everything that was going on in the hayloft, where the back part was already stacked high with hay. She could make out the outlines of Lawrence and Francis as they pitched the hay here and there, high up in the mow. She could relay messages from the boys inside to Daddy and Angie outside.

"Coming up," she called as the next bundle of hay was on its way to the big opening. "On the track!" she shouted as it moved back. "Now," she called to Daddy when the bundle was over the spot it should be. Then he could trip the lever with his rope. Back and forth she called, warning the boys when to get out of the way because another bundle was arriving.

"Gee whiz, it's so dark up here I don't know where I'm spreading the hay," grumbled Francis.

"Yeah," agreed Lawrence. "Aren't those haywagons empty yet? Is this the last bunch coming up?"

"No, it is not," answered Anna Rose, but she did not speak loudly enough.

"What did you say? It *is* the last?" Lawrence repeated.

"No!" screamed Anna Rose as loudly as she could. The horses heard the sound, but they heard it as "Whoa," so they stopped. Daddy thought he heard "Now," so he tripped the rope, releasing the hay. Instead of falling to the part of the mow farthest back, the hay dropped with a whispery, crunchy sound right over the spot where Lawrence was standing, near the edge.

"Oof!" cried Lawrence as he went somersaulting backward down the wall of hay, tumbling and turning. With a bounce, he landed in a soft pile of hay.

"Did you get hurt?" asked Anna Rose.

Lawrence got up slowly. Hay was sticking out from his hair and from his clothes.

"You look like a scarecrow, tee hee!" Anna Rose could not help snickering.

"Is that so?" asked Lawrence as he started dusting himself off. "You said you were a little bird learning to fly but I think you are a little crow, and pretty soon I am going to give you a good scare." He moved toward Anna Rose.

"No, no! I'm a swallow, not a crow," shrieked Anna Rose.

"What's going on up there?" called Daddy. "We still have two or three forkfuls on the wagon. No time to be fooling around." Lawrence came to the doorway as Anna Rose danced away, so he could not catch her.

"Pa, we can't see where we are spreading up there near the rafters. Why don't we just haul the rest up and drop it in one pile? We can spread it tomorrow."

"All right," agreed Daddy. "I guess that won't hurt none."

Anna Rose hurried down the ladder and through the barn.

"I'm going to the house so Lawrence won't catch me," she said to herself.

Supper was very late that evening. Mama had finished the milking all alone. Millie helped her as much as she could. She had fed Virgie and Mary Elizabeth and put them to bed.

Anna Rose was walking toward the table to sit down when Lawrence came in. He had a small bunch of hay in his hand.

"Where is that crow I'm supposed to scare?" he asked. "Ah, here it is." He lunged at Anna Rose and started to tickle her with the hay. He tickled her under her chin, under her arms, on her bare feet, and on her belly.

"Say you're sorry," he ordered laughingly.

Anna Rose could hardly talk, she was giggling so hard. At last she gasped it out: "I'm sorry!"

"All right, little crow. Now you can eat your corn," chuckled Lawrence.

"I'm a swallow," said Anna Rose. But then she looked at the table where there were heaping platters of golden corn on the cob, hot and steaming.

"Oh, no. I *am* a crow. A big crow, and I'm hungry enough to eat all that corn," announced Anna Rose. She ate five whole cobs for supper.

School At Last

Mama was crying. Lawrence was going far away, to Tacoma, Washington. He had found a job there.

"Aw, Ma, don't cry. I'll write you letters. And I'll send money and nice presents at Christmas." Lawrence did not want Mama to cry. But it did not stop him from going. He kissed Mama and quickly got into the car. Daddy was taking him to the train station in Winona. No one wanted to go along this time. It was too sad. They would miss Lawrence and his mischievous tricks.

"Goodbye! Goodbye!" They waved to him until the car turned the corner at the gate, and could no longer be seen.

For a few days, everyone was sad. Mama kept busy,

sewing and stitching. She was finishing new dresses for Angie, Millie, and Anna Rose. The material was all the same plaid, but Angie's was blue, Millie's was green, and Anna Rose's was mostly yellow and brown.

"Come, let me try it on you," Mama beckoned to Anna Rose. The dress fit nicely. Long, puffy sleeves came to her wrists, and around the collar and down the front Mama had sewed rows of yellow rickrack. Two long sashes were sewn into the side seams, and tied in back to make a big bow.

"Now all I have to do is hem it," Mama sighed with relief. She pinned it up as Anna Rose stood on the table and slowly turned around. In less than an hour, the dress was ready.

"You can wear it to church on Sunday, and then again on Tuesday, when you start school."

It seemed as though Tuesday would never come, but at last it did. The girls were extra careful at breakfast not to get their dresses wrinkled or spotted.

"Do you want me to hitch up the horses?" asked Daddy.

"I can do it," replied Angie proudly. She had helped Lawrence and Francis so many times, she was sure she could do it alone now. She slid the harnesses over the horses' necks and fitted the bits into their mouths. It took about fifteen minutes to get all the straps and reins buckled and slid into place. She backed the team up close to the buggy, with the tongue in between the two horses. Attaching the traces to the whippletree, she picked up the reins, climbed up to the front seat, and brought the wagon around to the front of the house.

Millie climbed up next to Angie and Anna Rose sat in the back seat.

"You have to move down to the jump seat as soon as we pick up the others," Angie warned.

"I know," said Anna Rose. That was the rule they followed. The oldest ones in the front seat, next oldest in the back seat, and the youngest ones on the jump seat.

Up, up they went, climbing the steep hill that ended just where they turned right on to the main road. Around the curve they clip-clopped, and there were all the cousins, waiting eagerly. They were excited about the first day of school, too.

As soon as they were settled in their places, Angie clicked to the horses, gave them a light slap with the reins, and started off. Soon they came to Kaldunski's hill. It was steep and Angie had to hold the reins tight so the horses would not go down too fast. Anna Rose could not see from where she was sitting, but she was sure that Angie was nervous.

Crack! Bump! "Whoa!" Anna Rose heard a thudding noise and Angie's shout, both in the same moment. Before she could stand up and turn around to see what was happening, she was thrust hard against the back of the front seat. Next to her, Mary Ann and Sally Ann were clutching the seat just as hard as she was. The buggy was twisting from one side of the road to the other.

Crash! They came to a stop in a ditch at the side of the road. Imelda, Bernice, and Millie went flying over the front seat and landed in a grassy, bushy spot a few feet away.

"What happened?" Anna Rose asked.

Angie stood at the side of the buggy but did not bother to answer. Instead, she was calling out to Eddie, who was tearing after the team of horses as fast as he could run.

"Catch them! Catch them!" screamed Angie. But Eddie was no match for the team. They were scared and put on a burst of speed. Down the hill, along the marshy bottom stretch, and around a corner they disappeared.

Anna Rose still could not believe they were standing there in their best dresses, with the horseless buggy in the ditch, instead of rolling merrily along to school.

Angie turned to the girls who had been thrown out of the buggy by the crash. "Did you get hurt?" she asked. They were brushing themselves off and Anna Rose could see that Imelda was crying a little.

"Thank God, no broken bones, at least," exclaimed Angie. She looked shocked and scared. Millie and Bernice had landed on a soft patch so they were hardly bruised. Imelda landed on a hard spot, so she was more shaken up. Angie and Eddie had jumped off before the buggy crashed. They were not hurt at all.

"What happened?" repeated Anna Rose.

"I don't know myself," Angie said, looking bewildered. They watched their cousin Eddie trudge back up the hill.

"The horses are gone. They'll probably run all the way to Dodge." Eddie looked glumly at the buggy. "Just what I thought. The pin on the whippletree broke loose and that scared them. Are you sure you attached the pole to the neck yokes?" he asked Angie.

"Of course, I'm sure. I know how to hitch up horses as well as anybody," Angie defended herself.

"Well, there's nothing we can do except push the buggy back up the road to Uncle Roman's place. Maybe they can telephone to Dodge so someone can watch out for the horses there." Eddie did not sound too sure that it would work.

"What about school?" asked Anna Rose.

"Aunt Sophie can phone up and tell them what happened," Angie assured her.

"You mean we won't get to school at all today?" asked Anna Rose.

"Well, maybe if they find the horses in Dodge and we can get someone to bring them back, there will still be time to go." Angie spoke hopefully. She did not want to miss the first day of school, either.

They got behind the buggy, or held on to the sides, and pushed until they had it back on the road. It was not too hard then to push it back up the hill and into Uncle Roman's yard. Aunt Sophie came rushing out of the house.

"Land's sake, what happened to you? Where are the horses?" she cried.

Angie explained and as soon as Aunt Sophie made sure no one was hurt, except for bruises, she telephoned the school and then her oldest sister, Aunt Mary, who lived in Dodge. It took her a long time to explain what had happened.

"I wish she would hurry," thought Anna Rose. "The horses are probably past Dodge by now." At last, Aunt Sophie hung up the phone, and then they had to wait for Aunt Mary to call back.

It was after nine o'clock when the telephone rang. But it was not Aunt Mary calling from Dodge. It was Mrs. Stencil, calling all the way from Pine Creek. The horses had come trotting right up to their barn, and turned in to take the stalls they always took while they waited out the long school day. Mrs. Stencil had been worried, wondering what happened to the buggy with all the children in it. Now Aunt Sophie took a long time explaining the accident to Mrs. Stencil, and reassuring her that the children were safe and sound.

"We're never going to get to school today, I just know it," Anna Rose said to herself. She had waited all summer long for this day, and now it was spoiled.

Finally, Aunt Sophie finished talking to Mrs. Stencil, but she did not hang up. Instead, she spoke to Angie, with her hand over the mouthpiece.

"Do you want to take our team and buggy to Pine

Creek? Then you can tie your team to the back when you come home this evening. You'll have to stop in Dodge for a new pin and bolt for the whippletree, but you can do that on the way home.''

Angie agreed this was a good plan but she did not want to drive a strange team.

"I'll do it," offered Eddie. "I've driven Buck and Ginger for Uncle Roman before."

It took a while to hitch up the horses so it was close to ten o'clock before they could start out again. Aunt Sophie wanted Imelda to stay home because she was covered with bruises. But Imelda insisted she wanted to go to school.

"She better not ask *me* to stay home," thought Anna Rose, "because I won't. I'll walk to school if I have to."

Aunt Sophie said no more, but waved goodbye as they settled themselves in the buggy and set off once again.

They all held their breath as they drove down Kaldunski's hill. When they got to the bottom safely, they relaxed. Now the road was mostly level, except for two small hills when they got nearer to Pine Creek.

"At long last, I'm really, truly on my way to school," thought Anna Rose. And it was going to be an even better start than she had expected. "Imagine being able to tell my classmates about such an exciting adventure on the first day of first grade."

"Oh, no," she corrected herself. "The *second* day of first grade!"

Pronunciation Guide

PAGE 15

Śiwy koń, śiwy koń
shee-vee koñ, shee-vee koñ (correctly pronounced as though it were like the ñ in the Spanish word *mañana*; however, we pronounced it koyn)

Malowany sankie
mah-lo-vah-nee sahn-kyeh

Poja dem, poja dem
poh-yah dem, poh-yah dem

Do twója kochankie
doh tvoh-ya ko-hahn-kyeh

Byl to kot
bill toh koht

PAGE 36

pok-shee-vas
pokrzywas is the correct spelling for this word, which is pronounced pok-rzhee-vahs; however, we pronounced it pok-shee-vas

PAGE 42

Dupa
doo-pah

PAGE 102

ponchki
pączki is the correct spelling for this word, which is pronounced ponch-kee

PAGE 105

Dyngus, Dyngus, po dwa jaja
ding-oose, ding-oose poh dvah yah-yah

Nie chc chleba tylko jaja
nyeh khtseh hleh-bah till-koh yah-yah